The Clockwork Circus

A novel by Alex McGilvery

The Clockwork Circus

Alex McGilvery

Copyright Alex McGilvery 2022

ClockWork font Max Infield, XEROGRAPHERFONTS
 used with permission.

ISBN 978-1-989092-76-7

Celticfrog Publishing
Clearwater, BC

Chapter 1 — An Unwelcome Student

Frederick's heart started again. He gasped painfully, then stared up into the arrogant, icy blue eyes of Vassily Harnchev. This wasn't the first time Frederick had died, but was the longest Vassily left him dead yet.

"You should thank me, builder." He slapped Frederick's cheek. "One of these days, I may walk away and leave you to rot."

"Thank you, Sar Harnchev." Frederick rasped the words out past the raging anger he carefully kept hidden. The first time they played out this farce, Frederick had died three times before his gratitude met Vassily's standard for groveling.

"Don't be late for class, builder." Vassily stood and walked away.

Frederick's watch buzzed once on his wrist. Five minutes to recover, another five to get to the Academy and be in his seat before Professeur sauntered in to take attendance.

He lay on the hard cobbles, people walking past him without turning their heads. From this angle the grey buildings loomed over him, seeming about to fall. Frederick half wished they would and put him out of this misery.

"Why do you let him do that?" Katerin crouched beside Frederick and put her hand on his chest sending warmth through to his battered heart. It beat more regularly, and he could breathe normally. Her brow wrinkled. He hadn't decided if it was worry or disappointment.

"Why do you keep showing up to help me?" Frederick took Katerin's offered hand, and she pulled him to his feet.

"Let's say, I'm not a fan of the Harnchev family." She frowned, her deep brown eyes clouded before she shook her head and let go of his hand. "You need to move if you're going to keep to your schedule."

"You know about my schedule?" Frederick's heart banged in his chest for a different reason.

"How long have I been stopping to help you?" She patted the same cheek Vassily slapped and hastened away.

Frederick had followed her one time to watch her enter Michealla Aetheric Finishing School, the girl's version of the Academy, on the far side of the huge green space which formed the center of Lexburg. He once got lost in the band of forest walling one half of the park from the other.

The punishment for missing the first class was severe—ten soft lashes and then he had to run laps of the campus until he collapsed.

Today, like every other one since his punishment, Frederick arrived in plenty of time.

Vassily stood with his cronies at the main entrance to the Dimitriac Academy of Aetheric Excellence. The architecture reflected the bombastic name, looking like a cross between fortress and summer palace., Frederick went around to the back, where, Vassily informed him on his first day, servants and builders entered.

The halls held the lower rung students scurrying furtively to get to their seats before the higher ranked ones came to punish any they thought moved too slow for the honour of the Academy. Some of them sent hostile glances toward Frederick, calculating if they had time for a little torture of their own before they were required to be seated.

Frederick smiled and nodded at them, refusing to bend the rules about walking in the halls. They snarled back at him, but fearful of their own status, left him alone.

Frederick slipped into his seat, the first, as usual, befitting his place as the pariah of the academy.

Horselli came in soon after and came to sit behind him.

"I set my watch by the time you arrive." He never looked at Frederick when he spoke, but he couldn't resist the need to have someone to speak to. If it weren't for Frederick, it would be Horselli's heart stopping and starting at Vassily's will. Or perhaps not. Horselli, however weak he might be, was aetheric, unlike Frederick.

"I will endeavour to maintain my punctuality for your sake." Frederick pulled out his books and carefully arranged them for the rest of the students to accidentally knock from his desk. It kept them, if not happy, at least content they'd put him in place.

The morning ritual proceeded with his notes collecting the proper number of footprints and rips.

Professeur marched in and rapped the desk with his stick.

"Roll call."

Frederick stood and looked down.

"Frederick LeSille, present."

He sat immediately and kept his eyes on his desk while the rest of the class stood, clapping their heels together and announcing their presence and importance.

The lecture picked up where they'd left off yesterday, in the middle of the sentence as if they'd not retreated to their rooms or homes to lick their wounds.

"- golem is intended to do physical labour on behalf of its creator. The aetheric must be aware of the status shown by one's golems. Anyone can make a golem from stone—"

As if on cue, Vassily walked in, making his usual dramatic entrance, swinging his cloak off to fold it carefully to stow in his desk at the back of the room before sitting. The lecture continued without pause during his show.

"—can work with wood or other organic material. The highest level of aether is to work with living objects — b" *Such as builders.* Frederick's chest twinged. "— The more conscious the object the greater the amount of skill and power needed." The Professeur may have glanced ever so briefly at Vassily here. "It is forbidden to work on humans, unless they have been convicted of a crime and sentenced by Lord Mayor Harnchev to be slaves." The lecture droned on covering material they'd been learning since the year started a month ago. Frederick wondering if working aether dulled the mind so much they needed the endless repetition for it to sink into their heads. He'd learned the entire curriculum the first week, keeping his careful notes only for the amusement of his aetheric classmates.

The bell rang, and Professeur cut off his words as if the sound was a knife. Frederick wondered if he'd restart in the middle of the word; or repeat the first syllable again. He laid a bet with himself as the class left the room in the reverse order of their arrival.

"LeSille," The Professeur rapped Frederick on the shoulder with his stick. He did like to use it at least once in the class. "Why are you here? It is a waste of our time."

"Professeur," Frederick kept his eyes down so the man wouldn't see the fury in them. "It is not by my choice, but my guardian is following my father's wishes in the matter. If I could remove myself, I would." He shrugged with a carefully measured movement. Enough to earn another strike with the stick, but not sufficient to enrage the man.

"I will speak to the Warden," the Professeur repeated his part of the formula. Frederick had laid a bet whether the man had ever approached the warden, but with no way to know, he couldn't decide whether he'd won or lost. The warden was the only person in the school who terrified Frederick more than Vassily.

Having played out their daily ritual, the Professeur turned away allowing Frederick to leave. The timing was such that Frederick should have been unable to arrive before any other student to the practical part of their learning. He walked along the hall at a measured pace which would give the least chance of an instructor or upperclassman stopping him for a lecture. He pushed open the door to the washroom. It was the least favoured by other students as it was the furthest from the hub of the school. Frederick still checked as he did every day to be sure he was indeed alone, then took his watch from his wrist. It crawled like a beetle up to the single small window and worked the latch, then pushed the window open. Frederick jumped up to catch the sill, then lifted himself up and out the window. His watch closed the window after him, the latch falling into place as Frederick had modified it to do after the third day of his purgatory.

The Academy formed a square around a garden showcasing the upperclass student's attempts to work with live plants. Beams ran from one side to the other holding up the large glass panels protecting the garden from the elements. Frederick ran along the closest beam to the far side of the square. With the weather chilling he might need to adjust his path to prevent danger from ice on the greenhouse supports.

He couldn't re-enter the school as he left it, but an ornate column made climbing to the roof simple, then an architectural oddity of a recessed alcove which ran from roof to foundation made it easy to lower himself to the ground. He walked out, shielded from sight by a pair of cedars, to the path which left him only steps away from the testing ground.

Not one student had ever shown the slightest interest in how Frederick arrived, relaxed and unruffled before any of them. It supported his theory that aether destroyed their ability to think, or perhaps it was the absolute certainty that being aetheric, no matter how weak, made them better than a builder.

The rest of the students arrived and stood in formation, this time putting Frederick at the rear.

Each student stood in front of either a stone or piece of lumber. Only Vassily worked with a living shrub.

"Form your golem and have it step to the right." Lectura didn't carry a stick. He had a small golem of wood which stomped up and down the lines meting out punishment to students who failed at their task.

The boy beside Horselli miraculously formed a golem, but it stepped to the left instead of right. Either its creator had difficulty knowing which was which, or his golem was being disobedient.

After Lectura's golem whipped Frederick for his failure to accomplish any movement at all, it laid a lash on Horselli and a few other students whose work didn't meet Lectura's exacting standard.

"Golems resent their existence." Lectura spoke as he marched back and forth. "The aetheric must be disciplined and strong to force the material to their will. The closer the material is to life, the greater its resentment." He pointed at the students. "Failure to bend the creature to your will may have fatal consequence if you overreach your ability. More than one aetheric has died at the hands of their own work."

They continued until the sun stood high above them. Lectura's golem stood by Frederick and whipped him emotionlessly, but Frederick suspected the thing enjoyed its task.

Lectura held Frederick back when he dismissed the rest of the students and forced him to continue his futile efforts to bring the rock to life until it was too late for him to eat any lunch. Frederick didn't know if the man knew he was doing Frederick a favour by giving him a reason to avoid the student dining room.

The afternoon lecture was the only part of the day Frederick looked forward to. The wizened man who taught the class claimed no title but excoriated every student who came short of his expectations, which was the vast majority. Vassily never missed, and never earned the teacher's scorn, but the rest of the first-year students sat through the man's sarcastic comments as he attempted to drive the theory and history of aether into their collective heads.

Frederick carefully hid his fascination, making sure to create enough opportunity for derision. At the end of the day, he headed home.

The walk back to his rooms was uneventful as Vassily would be headed over to the girl's academy to make his conquest of the week. Frederick imagined him chatting up Katerin and his stomach churned. He had less than no chance of anything more than the pity-based relationship they had, but Vassily would kill even that.

If Frederick didn't know Vassily had trouble acknowledging the existence of anyone but himself, he'd wonder if the twit had a personal vendetta against him. Frederick shook his head. Vassily needed no reason but the first builder ever having the gall to attend the Aetheric Academy to be in his class.

His guardian's dwelling sat sandwiched between identical buildings but for the colour of the doors and what window coverings displayed. Frederick pushed through the grey painted door into the grey painted hall. If grey had a smell, it would be the combination of mustiness and cleaner the housecleaner used.

Upstairs, he changed into the canvas and leather clothes which formed his work outfit. No one else was home, so he crept down to the basement, then activated the door he'd built to hide his shop. Not a single person had ever descended to the basement, never mind showed interest in the odd disparity between the size of the first floor and the lower one. Certainly not his guardian, Granfle, a large florid man who spent his day in the courts as a lawyer and acted in his role in name only, rarely even speaking to Frederick except occasionally to remonstrate him in vague terms to stay out of trouble.

If dying every day on the way to school was trouble, Frederick was failing miserably. He took off his watch and wound both springs before setting it on a post overlooking the worktable. Unlike a golem, the watch had no will. It only responded to the actions built into it. The evenings of the first week of school had been a frantic effort to make the thing open and close a window. If he'd been able to fit a third spring into it, he might make more use of it.

Pieces of clockwork scattered across the worktable. He had a contract to build a dancer for an aetheric child who would probably wind it up once, then break it. Frederick carefully assembled the doll-sized figure.

He could have put it together in his sleep, but the slightest error could lose him, not only this contract, but any to follow. The notoriety of his attendance at the academy gave him a brief cachet with the elite, who could point, even remotely to him, and remind themselves how much better they were.

Dreams of building figures to wield swords and axes to wreak havoc on the pestilential upper class filled his mind. Useless, worse than useless, as the aetheric would only warp the metal out of shape or make golems of the cobbles to destroy them and him. His watch only survived because he'd meticulously made it appear to be a simple timepiece. In truth, the true purpose took up so much space the thing made a barely adequate watch.

The dancer performed gracefully on his table. Frederick made minute adjustments, then wound it again. By the time he'd satisfied himself it was adequate, his eyes were barely staying open.

Upstairs to his room, a brief wash, then he fell on his bed. Tomorrow, he had another day in purgatory.

He should have been calling it Hell, but a tiny part of him refused to admit his father didn't have a reason for the torture. If he ever met the man, he'd ask, if he could keep himself from strangling him first. He also felt, for some insane reason, a desire to show up the aetherics by surviving.

As usual, vague nightmares troubled him, grey visions of a man who he recognized as his father, though he couldn't remember the man's face any longer.

***

The next day was a repeat of the last, the only exception being they had a rest day following. Frederick spent the rest day in his workshop making up spring and cogs. The more variety he had to work with, the more complex his creations could be.

The bell rang warning him someone waited at the door. Frederick ran up, took a long breath to steady his voice and opened the door.

A man in the Lord Mayor's livery stared down his nose at Frederick and begrudgingly handed him a folded square of paper of such quality its cost would have bought Frederick's meals at the academy for a week, were he allowed to eat them.

The man spun and stalked back to the waiting small coach without ever saying a word. A servant he might be, but he wasn't a builder.

The school had no need to teach the history of the builders, nor how they reached above their station. Sure, that had been a century before, but the memories of the aetheric were long when it came to their pride.

Frederick opened the paper. As he'd both expected and dreaded, it held a commission from the Lord Mayor to build a simulacrum to move as a soldier. At least the thing would present a welcome challenge since it was to perform the first four movements of attack and defense with the sword. It would need four springs. Frederick had only attempted it once before, and it had been a disaster, exploding in his shop embedding pieces in wall and flesh with equal abandon.

He closed the door, locked it, then walked to the library. The first step would be understanding exactly as possible the movement without actually studying the sword, something forbidden to builders for a hundred years. Frederick would have cursed his ancestors for their hubris, but it was a waste of time. It would be like expecting a new action from a clockwork after it had been completed.

"Are you sure?" The librarian frowned at Frederick. "It comes perilously close to breaking the ban."

Frederick handed her the paper.

"The Lord Mayor commands it."

She handed the paper back as if it burned her and directed him to the manuals with a stern reminder that he himself could not use the learning, even in a closed room with a stick.

He didn't need the reminder, the last builder to contravene the law ended up as a mindless slave, and that poor woman had only been carrying a wooden sword for a reason no one ever discovered.

The manuals were, like the lectures at the academy, overly repetitive. Here, it was a blessing. Frederick spent the afternoon studying the first four movements and only those out of the many, many actions which could be taken. He was sure the librarian lurked, watching nervously. There would be no telling what punishment the Lord Mayor would visit on the person to aid a builder in breaking the ban.

At closing time, Frederick had fixed the movements so solidly in his mind he would have to take care not to use them unthinkingly.

Leaving the books for the librarian to return to their shelves, Frederick walked reluctantly to the doors. If Vassily had so much as caught a whiff of his father's commission, he'd be there, waiting.

The shadow of the Lord Mayor's son leaned against a wall. Only the sword at his waist caught the sun. They did not teach the art of the sword at the academy. It was assumed each family would train their offspring against the possibility of another uprising where they might have to lift their own hands in defense.

In reality, it led to many duels between bored young men. If they didn't kill each other, aether would remove any injury or scar. The only legitimate use of aether on another human, even a builder. Vassily had explained, the first time he killed Frederick, that he was training in the healing arts and Frederick was his lucky test subject.

No use in waiting, it would only annoy the boy, spurring him to greater efforts in the exploration of the line between life and death.

Frederick tucked the commission away and marched to his doom.

"You have been studying the sword." Vassily didn't waste time with small talk. He drew his sword and pointed at Frederick.

"I have been studying movement for a commission." Frederick didn't bother mentioning it was the Lord Mayor's commission.

Vassily didn't bother replying, but came at Frederick with the first attack, a lunge to the heart. The book stated categorically the defense was to dodge away from the attack and riposte. Frederick moved into the sword catching the blow early so it scraped across his ribs instead of piercing his heart.

Sar Harnchev whipped the blade out and around to the second attack a slash at the throat. Here he should move back and use the sword to guide the opponent's blade away from one's body. Frederick ducked, but not fast enough, probably why the book didn't recommend it. The tip of the sword opened Frederick's left cheek from nose to ear. Hot blood flowed down his face. The taste of iron filled his mouth.

Pain should have been Frederick's response to the injuries. He should have screamed in agony, fallen to the pavement, begged for his life. Instead, he put his hand to his face and took it away bloody, then flicked the red liquid at the Lord Mayor's son, staining his undoubtedly expensive clothes.

The response was immediate and predictably brutal. Vassily's sword whistled through the air, becoming invisible. It struck Frederick's left leg just above his knee. He was shocked it didn't hurt more. His attacker spun and stomped away, brushing at his shirt.

Frederick didn't realize his leg had been cut off until he tried to take a step and fell to the cobblestones. The shock of his landing released the pain which had been absent. He bit his cheek to hold in his scream. Frederick lay writhing on the street while bystanders made a careful detour around him. Any who'd witnessed the incident would be eager to distance themselves from the Lord Mayor's anger.

"Hsst, lie still." Warm hands flitted across his body stealing away the agony and leaving behind lethargy. Katerin's eyes flashed. Frederick thought he was delirious, as green lighting danced behind her pupils. "I can stop the bleeding and ensure you live, but even I can't reattach what is lost, not without..." She shook her head. "Even you don't deserve this."

"Thought you liked me," Frederick mumbled as if drunk and couldn't stop his words. "Why else would you watch over me?"

"You are my sworn enemy." Katerin spoke with such heat he had no choice but to believe her.

"Why?"

"There are worse things than enemies." She stood and walked away leaving him with only the company of his severed leg.

Chapter 2 The Price of a Leg

The city guard showed up, likely in response to complaints that he blocked the street. They hoisted him up and carried to their barracks.

"What happened?" The man asking had stripes on his sleeve which blurred and blended so Frederick couldn't count them. He needed to know how many stripes there were, but he couldn't ask.

"My leg fell off." Frederick giggled.

"Legs don't just fall off." The man with the blurry stripes shook Frederick.

"Depends on who makes them fall." Another man leaned against the wall. His sleeve had no markings, so he wasn't interesting to Frederick. "You will not find anything against that one. It is dangerous to try."

"No one should be above the law." Blurry stripes sounded like he was in pain, but he still had both legs.

"This is the real world, and ideals like that will get you killed." No stripes pointed at Frederick. "Send him home; and count yourself lucky he's delirious." He pushed away from the wall and came to stare into Frederick's eyes. "I am curious who healed him. He should have died, even the Lord Mayor's healer might have struggled to keep him alive."

"My sworn enemy." Frederick brushed at the tears pouring from his eyes. When had they started?

"Your enemy saved you?" Blurry stripes stood up and stormed out of the room.

"I'm guessing you don't mean the Lord Mayor's son."

"Worse than an enemy." Frederick held his hand to his face, then the room whirled around him. Strong arms kept him from falling. Distant voices argued, but finally rough hands picked him up and pitched him onto a bed. A cloud of foul dust enveloped him.

"Drink or die." The clank of a tin cup accompanied the statement. Frederick spilled more than he swallowed, but the voice didn't complain.

***

Frederick woke and thought his nightmare worse than usual. Then he saw the bars closing him in. His hands flew to his left leg, it ended too early, truncated, making him a cripple. Perhaps Vassily had finally achieved his goal of exorcizing the builder from the academy. At least he would leave Frederick alone now. Ironic that Vassily wielded the sword and Frederick was behind bars.

"Awake now, are you?" A rotund man with a belt hanging with keys came and stared through the bars.

"Why am I here?" Frederick tried to put together the course of events after the loss of his leg. He could remember eyes flashing with impossible green light. His sworn enemy, but the rest of face eluded him. That was his last memory before waking in this cell.

"Couldn't hardly let you die after someone went to all the trouble of saving your life." The man pulled the gate open. "Come on, get a bite to eat before you go."

"How am supposed to walk?"

The man pointed to a crutch leaning against the wall.

"Had it lying around." He shrugged. "Better get used to it."

Frederick picked up the crutch and hopped awkwardly along the corridor.

"What time is it?"

"Not yet first bell."

"I must go, or I'll be late to class."

"You must be joking." The rotund guard stared at Frederick.

"No." Frederick swung along, in too much of a hurry to wonder at the lack of pain. For the first time since he'd started at the academy, Vassily didn't wait for him at the crossroads before the magnificent park. He glimpsed movement; but didn't stop to wonder about it. His entire being focused on getting to the academy and his place in class.

As he moved Frederick became more practiced with his crutch, increasing his speed. He didn't consider how to stop until he slammed into the back door of the academy.

"I'm going to have to come up with something better than that."

Frederick rubbed his nose, and his fingers brushed over a scar. He followed it to his ear. There would be another one on his ribs. They didn't feel fresh, but old and hard. Another time, he'd worry about it.

With some careful maneuvering, he got the door open and went through it. The hall went still as he thumped his way to the first class. No one looked at him, but none looked away either.

His seat in the front of the room was a welcome relief. In his obsession, he hadn't noticed the effort needed to move, but as soon as he sat, exhaustion hit him.

Horselli came in.

"I was sure my watch was off, but here you are." He waved at Frederick's lack of a left leg. "What?"

"It fell off." Frederick looked up at the other student, daring him to take umbrage.

Horselli opened his mouth, closed it, then opened it again.

"Are you all like this?"

"All who?" Frederick raised his eyebrow.

"Builders." Horselli sputtered. "Are you all insane?"

"Just me." Frederick looked to the door as the next students filed in. "Why else would I be here?"

Muttering filled the room, but no one else approached him.

Professeur came in as usual.

"Roll call."

Frederick pushed himself upright and balanced on his one leg as he looked the shocked man in the eye. "Frederick LeSille, present." He glanced down and grinned wryly. "Mostly." He sat with a thump and the roll call staggered on.

The Professeur picked up the lecture, stumbling over his first words.

Vassily swept in looking, if possible, even more smug than usual. Then he saw Frederick and paled like someone had slapped him. He stalked over to Frederick, hand twitching at his waist as if searching for a sword.

"What happened to your leg, builder?" Something burned in his eyes as he licked his lips.

"It fell off." Frederick thumped it. "Careless of me, I know." He shrugged as if it was little concern. "I'll get by."

Vassily turned red and his hand clenched. He wanted Frederick to accuse him. It would cement his reputation as an untouchable terror.

"I thank you for your concern." Frederick nodded his head. A strange noise came from Vassily.

"Master Harnchev, I would like to continue my lecture." Professeur spoke mildly, but Vassily's head snapped around as if he'd been whipped. Then he strode to his seat, tossed his cloak over the back of the seat, and slumped in the seat.

The lecture continued its inevitable path, and since Frederick didn't have his books, he couldn't take notes. He sat straight and watched attentively. Several times Professeur glanced in his direction and stuttered before regaining his rhythm. At the close of the lecture, he left the room without singling Frederick out for a lecture on his incompatibility with the academy.

Frederick humped himself upright and headed out of the class. The other students moved out of his path as if he might be dangerous.

The lesson with Lectura went the same way. The class waited for Lectura to ask about Frederick's leg, but either the man didn't notice, or more likely had heard the story through the grapevine.

The golem came as usual to punish Frederick for his failure to achieve the impossible. Frederick moved his crutch slightly to block the thing's blows. It didn't notice or perhaps it didn't understand the difference. The clack of wood on wood rang through the air like an offbeat drummer. Eventually the golem waddled away to punish those who had let distraction affect their efforts.

Frederick hopped away with the rest of the class. Lectura paid no heed.

What am I going to do for lunch?

He had no choice but to brazen it out. Vassily was one thing, but the upperclassmen were a law unto themselves, and even Sar Harnchev steered clear of their disapproval.

"Here." Horselli patted the seat beside him. "Tell me what really happened. I mean, you didn't have that scar yesterday."

"Really?" Frederick ran his fingers along the line. "I thought I'd always had it."

"You, builder." A figure with the black sash of an upperclassman loomed behind them.

Frederick turned and bowed as best he could, trapped beside Horselli, who looked ready to crawl under the table.

"Stand up."

He clambered to his feet balancing on his one leg with a hand on Horselli's shoulder for support.

"What happened to your leg?" The upperclassman's eyes glittered coldly.

"It fell off, Sar Classman."

"Legs do not just fall off." His hand dropped to the short baton which was the reason for the sash.

"How I wish that were true." Frederick forced his face into a mask of dejection.

"And where is it then, this leg that fell off?"

"I wish I knew, Sar Classman. It certainly has made no attempt to find me."

The upperclassman's brow wrinkled, and Frederick was sure he'd earned a beating. Then the other student burst into laughter and turned away to joke with those who stood around him. He had to be the upper class version of Vassily, but perhaps with a little more humanity. Vassily sat staring at Frederick as if he'd been turned to stone. Frederick turned back to the table. Horselli handed him a sandwich.

"I was about to fill my pants. Sar Mitryi thrashed a student once because he wore the same shirt as him." He lowered his voice. "He's the Warden's son."

"He seemed like a reasonable gentleman." Frederick bit into the sandwich.

***

For the next week, Frederick was a bit of a celebrity. He never wavered from the story that his leg had simply fallen off. Occasionally he hinted it was out there carousing without him, but more in sorrow than in anger.

Vassily ground his teeth in fury, but with the upperclassmen finding Frederick amusing, there was nothing he could do without risking their ire at spoiling the fun.

As Frederick quit acting like he didn't belong, many of the lower ranked students, like Horselli, gathered around him to bask in whatever small glory he carried.

The fuss died down over the following week with more and more students distancing themselves as the upperclassmen found other amusements. Many students looked nervously at Vassily who glowered at everyone equally.

The first day of the third week, Frederick's crutch twisted in his hand, dumping him on the floor. Heat burned in Frederick's gut, but he tamped it down and smiled at Vassily who stood looking triumphant.

"I was wondering how long it would take you to figure it out." Frederick pushed himself up and held his crutch in front of him, then he shrugged and continued down the hall. Each time the crutch moved, he held it away from him and hopped.

All week Vassily laid in wait to make Frederick fall. Frederick's fury built as his newfound status slid back to pariah. On the last day, Horselli came and sat down without speaking to him. His descent was complete.

He'd barely made it home before someone knocked the door.

"The Lord Mayor is disappointed you failed to complete his commission." The messenger swiveled and walked back to the coach.

There would be no more commissions. No one would dare contract with a person who had displeased the Lord Mayor.

Frederick hopped down the stairs to his workroom. All the parts carefully lined up, ready for use, worthless. He screamed and overturned his table then scattered the springs and cogs across the floor.

When he'd quit in exhaustion, he sat in the room playing with a brass plate. If only clockwork wasn't limited to four springs, he'd destroy Vassily. Clockwork or not, the boy would pay, there had to be a way.

Chapter 3 A Sworn Enemy

Katerin watched as Frederick moved up from his place at the bottom of the social ranks; the subject of gossip for the girls at her school. Some even talked more about Frederick than Vassilly. It didn't last, it couldn't, Frederick was a builder, and the social norms would be restored. As he grew more bitter, she wondered if she'd done him a favour by saving his life.

She hadn't thought about it. Vassily intended Frederick to be maimed but most likely he expected the builder to bleed to death on the street. Vassily infuriated her. A long string of broken-hearted girls wept in the dining room after he'd finished with them. Some disappeared and were not spoken of, as if they'd never existed.

The builder should have stayed at home, content to have survived his foray into far too rarified air for his kind. She knew about being with people who were not her own. Watching Frederick had been an exile of sorts, one she didn't want or understand.

Then she watched his face as even the place he had was destroyed. Katerin's heart almost broke as Frederick received his punishment, then closed the door eyes showing pain the rest of him denied. When smashing and howling came from the basement where he worked, she couldn't stand it anymore.

The streets blurred as tears leaked from her eyes. Healing him had been a monstrous act. She was responsible for his agony. No one deserved what he'd withstood, enemy or not.

Her feet knew the path and carried her faithfully to where the gloom of a back alley become the Stygian night of her queen's court. Katerin stopped and took hold of her runaway emotions, throttling them and pushing them away. They had no place here.

Katerin's gut ached, and traitorous eyes still watered, but it would have to do. The guards nodded at her but didn't speak. She breathed a little easier. At least they had not barred her from court.

People turned to watch her enter, the softest of murmurs flowed through the room. The queen sat at her chair, scratching a dog behind the ears. Harmo's mouth gaped open, and his eyes rolled in overwhelming pleasure.

"Greetings, daughter." The queen looked up without stopping her fingers. "I have missed you."

"You were the one to send me away, Mother." Katerin couldn't stop the bitter edge to her voice. "Three months in their world, and I have no more idea of why than before." Her voice caught. "They do such horrible things to each other in the name of pride." Volcanic grief flowed from her deepest being. "And yet I did the worst. I healed our enemy, and left him to suffer brief hope, then bitter destruction." She lost her battle to keep her emotions at bay. "Why did I save him?"

Katerin fell to her knees sobbing. Harmo licked at her face, then a soft hand caressed her cheek.

"My daughter, you healed him because you are a healer, and of all people, he needs healing."

"You said he was our enemy." Katerin hiccupped and hugged Harmo.

"I said he would betray us." The queen lifted Katerin's chin. "That is different."

"How can you say that, if he betrays us, does that not make him our enemy?"

"The augury was as strange as it was powerful. Frederick LeSille would betray us, but I felt as strongly as I have ever done, that he needed to be watched and perhaps protected."

"Will the augury change if we watch him?"

"No." The queen sighed and lifted Katerin to her feet. They stood eye to eye.

When did she grow so small?

"Ask rather, when did you grow so tall." Her mother's mouth twitched. "It is hard to see one's child grow. The day will come when you will surpass me."

"Father is not that tall." Katerin sucked in as much air as she could hold, letting it steady her.

"I'm not talking just height." Her mother led her to the chair and sat Katerin in it. The crowd rustled as they went to their knees. "You are my heir, and the hope of our people."

Katerin stared at her openmouthed. "But I don't understand!"

"Nor do I." Her mother played with Katerin's hair. She had once delighted in molding Katerin's long hair into fantastical shapes. "To rule is not always to understand, but to live in ambiguity."

The side door to the hall opened and Katerin's father strode it.

"I had word that Katerin ha—" He broke off mid-word and went to his knee.

"Father, no." Katerin reached out her hand, then let it drop lifeless in her lap.

"It is my great joy to see my daughter take the throne." He lifted his head to reveal a broad grin. Katerin ran to him. His powerful arms held her until she stopped shaking.

"But why?"

"Why now?" Her mother resumed her seat. "You are our hope and ambassador in the outer world. It is vital you know you have the absolute support of your people." She tilted her head. "I will rule as regent until you know it is time to claim your place."

"But..." Katerin turned around in a circle taking in the kneeling people. They were her teachers, the parents of her friends. "I accept. I will be your queen if you will have me."

They stood and smiled, then mobbed her to congratulate and advise her.

***

"You certainly picked an effective way to derail my questions." Katerin eyed her mother over the table. Her father spread butter on a roll and rolled his eyes.

"Questions." Her mother sighed and leaned back in her chair. "If only I had answers. I sent you to watch him partly to assuage the augury, but also because we need to know the temper of the outer world."

"No one speaks our name. We aren't even bogeys to scare children." Katerin frowned. "It is as if we were erased from memory."

"You understand my thought." Her mother played with her fork. "We have been alternately sought or feared. Being forgotten is new and troubling."

"Why troubling? Isn't it better if they don't know we are here?"

"Better for now." Katerin's father rumbled. "But what happens when they learn again, we are here? They may blame us for making them forget."

"But..." Katerin fell silent as thoughts tumbled through her head, she gasped as they clicked into place and horror filled her.

"Fear is a powerful tool for those who sit uncertainly in their place."

"The ban on the builders." Edges of ideas ground and cut her mind. So much pain she could hardly see.

"Someone is using Frederick to catalyze hate against them. When they are gone, they will need a new enemy." She held her head as if it might crack. "Survival lies beyond..." Agony stole her consciousness and she fell to the floor.

"I never told you the auguries were such agony." Her mother knelt holding Katerin's hand. Her father held the other. "Perhaps I did you a disservice."

"I wouldn't have believed you." Katerin used her parents' hands to pull herself upright. "I don't know what I saw at the end."

"That is the nature of auguries, they reflect possibilities, opportunities."

"But not answers." She stood and lifted her parents. "I still don't understand." Katerin felt her lips twist in a smile. "I must return to the other world before school begins, but that leaves us a little time to be as a family without dire hopes to haunt us."

***

Returning to school in the outer world was as painful as Katerin expected. This world was filled with harsh light and jagged edges. Cruelty lay just under the surface. But her friends grabbed her hands and babbled on about their day off, which boys they'd seen from a distance. They linked elbows with Katerin and smiled when she told them she'd visited her family.

"It did you good." Mischa held Katerin at arm's length. "You look more settled. I worried, you were so distant last week."

"I had some troubling things to work through. My parents helped."

"As they should," Akilina said. "Isn't it their job to help us find answers?"

"Say perhaps, to live with our questions."

The girls laughed. "Now we know you're back, you're not making any sense at all."

Katerin laughed with them and headed into the school. This afternoon she'd catch up on Frederick, but she feared he'd be caught in despair in his rooms.

She walked toward his rooms; and saw him thumping along with a twisted crutch. He looked at her and it might have been a knife stabbing her through the heart. His eyes glittered harshly, and a cloud hung over him which made her shudder.

"Hello Katerin." Frederick came over to her. "It is good to see you, but I need no healing now, but thank you from the bottom of my heart for what you have done for me."

Katerin's heart ached. *He remembers me healing him on the street? I was sure I clouded those memories.*

"Without your aid when Vassily played with my life, I would not have had the strength to survive."

"I, I am glad to have helped." Katerin fumbled out the words, still confused.

"But I must suggest it would be wise for you to keep your distance now. It wouldn't be good for you to be seen with me."

"Not everyone despises builders." Katerin protested, reaching her hand out.

"True," Frederick nodded sharply. "But they despise me." He turned and hopped away his crutch hardly any help at all.

Katerin stood watching him, shaking like a leaf. He may have been an enemy, but she never feared him as a person. Not until now.

What have I done?

Chapter 4 An Impossible Thing

Frederick put Katerin out of his mind as soon as she was out of his sight. He'd felt the need to thank her, but he didn't need pity anymore.

He went straight downstairs and changed into his work clothes. The workshop had become his home.

The thing on the table mocked him. It was impossible, there were too many movements, even with such a large creation he couldn't fit the necessary springs into it. He clenched his fists and stepped back before he destroyed it. The solution didn't lie in this room.

Not bothering to change out of his work clothes, Frederick headed away from his rooms. He deliberately pushed the problem out of his mind. The air was growing chill as winter approached. That would be a new level of hell if he couldn't work out the issues.

A poster caught his eye. Garish letters proclaimed the coming of the Clockwork Circus. A man in a grey coat and wearing a top hat, all of it covered with gears. Behind him loomed enormous shadows, if they were clockworks, they were bigger than anything he'd ever imagined. Here were builders not ashamed to claim what they were. Frederick grinned, probably much of their success had to do with the aetheric's urge to own clockworks for their children.

According to the poster it was arriving on the next rest day and would be here for an undetermined time. *Long enough to mine every coin they could from the aetherics.*

Frederick returned to his home and pushed his project to one side and buried himself in his work adjusting springs and cogs. He had an idea to move forward on his primary goal.

At the academy he sleepwalked through the week, ignoring all Vassily's efforts to torment him, except for handing the now useless crutch to the aetheric.

"You might as well have this; you enjoy playing with it so much."

Vassily's hands twitched, but he had to restrain himself with others watching him. The grinding of his teeth made Frederick cheerful. While Frederick had plunged to the depths, he'd started there, and there wasn't much worse they could do to him. Vassily had never recovered the height of his popularity. The Warden's son Mityri, a second-year student, challenged him at every turn.

"You're pushing your luck." Mityri murmured behind Frederick. "I tolerate you annoying him, but I will not protect you."

"I do not ask you to." Frederick spoke without turning around.

"My father will not tell me why you are allowed to sully these halls."

"Perhaps an enemy of *my* father has enough influence with the Warden to send me to hell."

"This is the most prestigious school in the city."

"And I am a *builder*." Frederick snarled the word. "What would you call a place where everyone hates you on principle?" He hopped away, practiced enough from dodging Vassily's plays with his crutch to stay upright and not wobble.

The only downside of giving the crutch away was the golem had no barrier between his blows and Frederick.

"Just die, won't you?" Frederick whispered harshly. The golem stared up at him, then grinned, showing teeth to make a wolf nervous, before it fell to the ground and decomposed into a pile of wood and rocks.

Lectura sprinted over and yelled at Frederick.

"What did you do?" He pointed at the remains. "Never interfere with another aetheric's golem. Never." The man lifted his hand to strike Frederick.

"I am not an aetheric." Frederick made his face stone. "In the months I've been here, have I ever made a rock so much as tremble?"

"Go, and don't come back. I don't care what the Warden says, I will not have you in my class." Lectura strode to the front. "I will say this once, though it should not need saying. Do not work on another aetheric's golem. You know they resist life, and the slightest error can free them. I will not ask who destroyed my work, but I will punish the lot of you." He glared at Frederick and pointed away.

He shrugged and hopped away. Would his father's strange hold on the Warden, or Lectura's rage win out? Frederick didn't care. He'd learned something unexpected. The golem listened to him, though he didn't have the slightest amount of aether in him.

Was it because Frederick was in the class, so it assumed he was aetheric? That didn't make sense, it implied a higher level of thought than the Professeur assigned to the things. One task of managing a golem was giving it detailed instructions, though the older ones learned some tasks. *How old was that golem?* Lectura never gave it an order, at least not verbally, but no one hinted at mental control of a golem.

Vassily said nothing when he stopped Frederick's heart, nor when he did any other work. The work of creating the creatures was mental, buy why did Lectura's golem need verbal commands? He sat in the dining hall ignoring everyone through lunch, only Horselli moving beside him jarred him out of his fugue.

"This is the most boring class." Horselli whined. "We don't need to understand how they work, that we can make golem is enough." He'd created his first, deformed but active golem just the day before. He'd dissolved it at the end of class as they were required. 'Your life is no longer needed.' was the phrase he'd used. All of them used some variant to dismiss their golems, except Vassily who waved his work into destruction. Again, words or not words?

They sat as the old man bombarded them with complex theories of how the golems worked and how to get the most out of them.

"Can you make a golem more intelligent?" Frederick's words came out before he could stop them. Every eye in the room focused on him. Since he'd started not one student asked a question of teacher. Even if they'd be allowed to use it, they didn't know his name, and he took no title to be addressed as. Speaking as Frederick had was the height of rudeness.

Frederick half expected to be kicked out of another class.

"It is forbidden, do not even think on it. Golems are golems and must remain so." The instructor stared balefully at the class. Every student nodded vigorously. The class continued, but at the end the instructor pointed at Frederick. "Stay."

He watched the students file out, some with puzzled expressions, some, like Vassily, smug.

"You are intelligent." The wizened man glared at Frederick. "That is dangerous."

"Intelligence is dangerous?"

"More than you know. We've been watching you. Don't force us to take action."

Frederick wanted to know who was watching, and what action, but he feared asking would precipitate the action.

"I will endeavour to be less intelligent from now on."

"Wise." The instructor walked away, leaving Frederick's mind spinning.

Intelligence dangerous? Why? The nature of the instruction at this school came to his mind. Repetitious far past the point of boredom. As least for Frederick. He'd never heard one student complain the classes were boring because they'd already learned it. Vassily was always late, and often left early, yet the teachers didn't complain.

There were three lessons.

Golems were useful and set the aetheric apart from the other people in the city. Yet he saw very few golems on the streets of the city.

Creating golems took careful thought and concentration. The slightest lapse would destroy the golem. Even months into the year, half the class still struggled to make anything but the most basic form. Again, Vassily was the exception, making whatever he pleased and having it dance to his tune.

No other student attempted to twist Frederick's crutch, not even the upper years who should have easily been able to manipulate it. The senior students used batons to enforce their will, not golems, which would have to be more satisfying.

Then there was the class on theory, the how and why. Vassily was never late, and he didn't lounge about as he did in the first class of the day. They were boring the entire student body in order to teach a select few what they needed to know. It had the side benefit of revealing students who could think beyond allowable limits.

"You are thinking." The old man glowered at him.

"Trying to figure how to appear stupid without being obvious about it." Frederick shrugged.

"Let your eyes glaze over, drool if you have to. No one will notice or care, except those who watch."

The Warden, the Lord Mayor, and a teacher with no use for grand titles.

Frederick hopped home deep in thought. Movement distracted him, Katerin walked on the other side of the road with two other girls. She always seemed to be around. He added her to the list of watchers.

***

Frederick had to restrain his eagerness to get out of class. Not that many students looked excited to be there. They were covering why golems were more difficult the closer to life the material started. Some material held aether, and some let it flow. Living things held aether in place, making it hard to force one's will on them.

Vassily had started and stopped Frederick's heart with aether, something about that danced on the edge of his consciousness, but the next bit almost made him sit bolt upright. A muscle in his back complained at the force with which he forced it still. Stone let aether flow. Aether flowed through metal without touching it, so it was all but impossible to work it into a golem. It could bend and twist, but not live.

The class ended, and Frederick joined the crowd fleeing the school. The Circus had been the talk of the school the entire week. Every student in the school would head there tomorrow. The watchers would be there, he would have to alter his plan. Frederick cursed his luck, but better safe than sorry.

Once again Katerin waltzed by with her friends. The idea leaped to mind fully formed and had him across the road before he could second guess himself.

"Fre Katerin, in gratitude for your kindness, I would like to invite you to the first day of the circus. I will pay, of course." Frederick bowed deeply, then stepped back to wait for her answer.

"Ugh," one girl said and looked at Frederick like he was a bug.

"Katerin, you can't, your reputation would never recover." The other one didn't pay any attention to him, holding both of Katerin's hands and shaking them.

"It is a builder circus, it might be amusing to attend with a builder. He'd be able to explain how things worked."

The two girls wrinkled their brows in thought.

"But Vassily..."

"All the more reason." Katerin pulled her hands from her friend. "I have no wish to end up as one of his conquests."

"But he's so handsome, and the Lord Mayor's son..."

"And such a kind person, you will say nothing of the rest day you spent with him." Katerin shook her friend. "Even now you are shaking."

The two girls fled, leaving Katerin staring after them.

"So, I guess I will meet you here a half bell before the Circus opens." Frederick caught something flicker through her eyes, but a headache struck him, and he looked at her wordlessly.

"I will be here." Katerin walked after her friends.

The headache faded as quickly as it came, leaving behind a single thought. Katerin was as intelligent as her friends were not. His certainty she was a watcher strengthened.

Tomorrow would be an interesting day.

Chapter 5 A Day with the Enemy

Katerin checked herself for the fourth time, then took a huge breath before opening the door to her room. A crowd of girls fluttered in the hallway, failing to hide their curiousity.

"Are you sure?" Mischa put her hand on Katerin's arm. "You could go with us later."

"And break an agreement?" Katerin raised an eyebrow. "I would keep my word to the lowest beggar, not for their sake, but because I gave it."

"But he's a *builder*." Akilina wailed.

"His blood is as red as ours, I've seen enough of it." Katerin threw the words at the girl and was rewarded by a shocked silence in the hall. *How do I get out of this mess?* She shuddered theatrically. "You have heard that Frederick lost a leg. I was coming out of the library when he was attacked."

"They say he claims it fell off." Mischa tilted her head. "But I can't see how that could happen."

"It fell indeed, but it had help."

"You saw it happen? Who..." Akilina paled. "It had to be a monster. My gran used to talk about monsters living under the city who'd steal the faces of people to commit horrible crimes."

Katerin almost grabbed the girl to shake the tales out of her, but she held herself back.

"Don't Akilina," Mischa frowned. "You're terrifying her, look how she shakes. Everyone knows your gran went mad."

Akilina put her hand to her mouth, then fled in tears.

"You'd better go and put things right." Katerin pushed Mischa after their friend.

"But it's true."

"Being true doesn't mean it needs to be said." She pushed harder. "Go."

"Yes, Katerin." Mischa ran after Akilina as Katerin scanned the rest of the flock with a gaze like a sword.

"Don't you ladies have something better to do?" They fled in clumps. Katerin sighed. *How do these people rule Lexburgh when they can barely rule themselves?* She'd have to walk much faster than the deportment instructor demanded if she was going to be on time. *Better to keep my word, then my dignity.*

***

Katerin stopped at the corner before their agreed meeting place. Frederick stood watching the passing crowds, his back to her. She closed her eyes and listened to her heart until it slowed. This builder was the key to her people's future, maybe their survival. He alternately terrified her and mystified her, and to be honest, she thought he'd be better company than the aetheric.

He turned and regarded her with a solemn expression. She wondered if his thoughts matched hers. He too was out of his natural environment; from what she'd learned he knew no more of the reason than she did.

"Good day, Fre Katerin." He bowed to her, balancing carefully on a new crutch.

"Let's get something straight," Katerin said, he frowned at her tone. "For this day. I am Katerin, and you are Frederick, nothing more."

"Yet we are what we are." His eyes were so dark as to be almost black, with just a hint of gold to define the pupil. She'd never paid attention to them before. They were arresting, and today without the shadow of violence she'd seen other times.

"For this day." Katerin smiled, trying to look friendly without being seductive. "And tomorrow we will be what we will be. But is not a circus a fantastical place? The rules of this world should not apply."

"Very well, Katerin." He smiled slightly and his eyes lightened.

"Well Frederick, shall we go?"

They walked side by side toward the large square the circus had claimed. Passersby stopped to stare, and more than one stumbled on the cobbles.

They made a strange pair; he wore plain canvas pants and a cotton shirt, clean, but only what a builder would wear any other day, hopping with the help of a crutch. Though her friends hadn't wanted her to come, they also wanted to dress as if for a ball. She'd resisted, but even what she thought of as a plain day dress looked fancy beside the utility of his garb.

They came to the gate of the circus. A high fence had been erected of wooden slats and covered with colourful posters to block the view of the inside. Two gatekeepers in bright red uniforms welcomed the people who line up down the street. Frederick stood in line with no comment.

An aetheric boy from Frederick's school and one of Katerin's upperclasswomen sauntered past the line. The boy dropped coins into a gatekeeper's hand, careful not to make any skin contact.

"Even here, the classes are divided."

"How else?" Frederick's words had an odd edge, not anger, but something. Katerin shook her head to clear her thoughts. "I am paying so we will enter as the common folk."

"We have all day." Katerin brushed a hand on his arm. "I will live in your world for a time."

He nodded but said nothing else.

Katerin watched as they crawled forward. Mothers bent over their children, encouraging them with tales of what they might find inside the walls. Young men stood with hands in pockets jingling change as if making sure they had enough. Couples held hands, in a world of the own.

"Aren't you fortunate to be escorting such a beautiful girl?" The gatekeeper grinned at Frederick as he put a hand out to receive coins.

Frederick turned to look at her as if he'd never seen her before. "Yes, I guess she is beautiful, but I am more interested in what she is inside."

The gatekeeper had already turned to the family waiting behind them.

Inside the gate, the noise prevented Katerin from asking what he'd meant. She wouldn't learn what she needed by questions anyway. The joyful chaos around her demanded her attention.

Clockworks were everywhere. They bobbed, spun, waved in a cacophony of action. Children laughed and squealed at their antics. Youth pretended to not be impressed.

Frederick examined them, nodding occasionally.

"What do you see?" Katerin waved her hand around her. Frederick cocked his head for a moment.

"They are well enough constructed, standardized parts for easy repair. Springs are designed to last a long time between windings, which is why they each only repeat one action."

"You could build them better?"

"I would build them differently, perhaps. I don't know about better. They are well suited for their task."

"But you are hoping to see wonders?" Katerin nudged him slightly.

"They will not have the wonders so close to the outside world." Frederick hopped forward, nimbly avoiding the crowd, using the crutch only for balance if a child ran in front of him.

Katerin kept pace, watching him as much as the scene about them. Vendors sold simple clockworks, but also hats, shirts and a bewildering number of other things. Who would come to a circus to buy shoes? Yet a man knelt to fit a shoe on an aetheric girl, a boy hovering protectively over her.

"They will appear to change shape as she walks. Her steps will set the springs to control the movement." Frederick peered at them until the boy frowned at him.

"How do you know these things?" Katerin asked, looking around for someone wearing the changing shoes.

"I'm a builder." Frederick stated and shook his head.

"But couldn't anyone put gears and springs together to make something?"

"Yes, they could, and it would work, but builders understand movements and how to transfer them into the simulacrum. We program them in ways other people could not." Frederick hunched his shoulders. "Centuries ago, builders created things to make the city work. Vehicles to carry people or freight, pumps to move water. Wonders we've forgotten how to make.

I can make a three-spring clockwork. Three distinct actions." He moved his hand to demonstrate. "When I was young, my father told me tales of clockworks with dozens of springs."

"Does your father still build clockworks?" Katerin bit her lip, her question could bite deeper than she intended.

"My father is gone. What he does?" Frederick flipped a hand. "I'm not sure I care any longer." He moved a little faster. Katerin swallowed her other questions.

As they walked, she saw they had constructed the Circus as a maze. Booths formed streets; small alleys led to shadowed tents. Frederick frowned. Only men strolled down those alleys, carefully casual.

They passed the vendors and the alleys to come on a large courtyard filled with immense machines which whirled and dipped as the people riding them scream in either delight or fear.

"Here is a wonder." Frederick stopped to stare.

"They only have one movement, most of them anyway, like the ones at the gate." Katerin examined them, trying to see what Frederick did.

"It isn't the complexity. You're right, they're simple enough, but the size. The springs must be huge, and the power..." He touched a tiny scar on his temple. "I can't imagine how they'd control it."

"They're dangerous?" Katerin stepped back.

"Everything is dangerous." Frederick grinned at her. "They wouldn't be here if the builders didn't know what they were doing." He tugged at her arm. "Let's ride one."

"Get on... that?" Katerin swallowed.

"You wanted to see the circus." Frederick pointed at the machines. "That's the circus."

Katerin scanned the rides until she saw one which moved slowly, a giant wheel on edge making a grand circle with no jarring turns or bumps. "That one." She pointed.

"Very well." Frederick led her to the lineup. Again, aetherics walked past as if other people weren't there. The people in their turn ignored them.

"It is as if they live in different worlds."

"Don't we?" Frederick looked at eyebrow raised. "You in the aetheric, working wonders, and the rest of us..." he shrugged slightly. "The rest of us living to be impressed."

"You don't sound impressed."

"I have seen deeper into the aetheric world than most; and found it hollow." Frederick spoke as if he was alone talking to himself. "At least builders create things with purpose."

They arrived at the front of the line. A man in a blue uniform took their money, then escorted them to hop onto a slowly moving cage with one bench.

"Don't be leaning on the door." The man closed it, and it latched with a click.

Katerin slid further from the door, heat from Frederick came through her dress. She almost moved back, but the memory of the conversation in the hall of her dorm came to mind and she stayed.

The wheel creaked and groaned as it lifted them high above the circus. Katerin looked down and gulped. Between gaps in the boards, only wire mesh contained them. The cage rocked gently. Katerin peered out the side, then slid closer to the door to see to that side.

"I won't let you fall." Frederick said.

She turned to look at him and saw he looked at her instead of the view.

"Isn't the view amazing?" She knew she babbled, but her insides were flopping uncomfortably. "I've never been this high before."

Not only the streets of the circus, but those of the city spread below them. They were broad in this section, though the carts she saw didn't need the space.

"What marvels moved in those streets?" She didn't realize she spoke out loud until Frederick answered.

"That is one reason I am here. The circus comes from elsewhere. Maybe from places where builders aren't reviled, and cities are still filled with movement and magic."

"Magic?" Katerin asked, not looking up.

"You didn't think clockworks were just copper and brass? We put something else into them, almost life. Like you aetherics make golems."

"That is how golems work, they are tortured fragments of what they could be." *What am I saying?*

The cage lurched to a stop and swung violently. Katerin grabbed hold of Frederick and squealed. He held her firmly, but impersonally. Her heart pounded from fear, then as they didn't fall to the far away ground, she relaxed.

"What happened?"

"The spring needs winding." Frederick pointed down to where several men in grey were walking in circles around a capstan.

"You knew this was going to happen!" Katerin sat up, her face flaming.

"Suspected." Frederick tilted his head and his lips twitched. "They built it for couples after all. Nothing like a bit of delicious fear to bring people together."

Katerin sputtered, not sure what to say, then she started laughing. "If my dorm mates could have seen me, a month ago they would have been jealous, now they'd be appalled."

"Jealous?" Frederick reddened slightly.

"Didn't you know? When you came to school claiming your leg had fallen off to wander without you. The girls were quite curious about you and what a builder would be..." Katerin stumbled to a stop. Some of the speculation had been very specific. Frederick blushed more and closed his eyes.

"It's as well I didn't know, just one more thing for me to lose."

Katerin put her hand on his. "It isn't fair, what they did to you."

"Which 'they'?" Frederick pulled his hand away and rasped his words bitterly. The shadow in his eyes had returned, and only the warning about the door kept Katerin from pushing against the wall of the cage to get away from him. "The ones who sent me without asking me to that school, knowing the hell it would be? Those who are all too happy to create that hell? Maybe those who use the school for their own ends and are trying to fit me into their schemes?" He snapped his mouth shut as if he regretted his last words.

"All of them, I don't know." Katerin grabbed him again as the wheel moved suddenly to begin its slow turn.

"You aren't aetheric." Frederick's eyes caught hers and wouldn't let her look away. "You play the role well enough for the dimwitted elite who populate the schools. I thought you might be one who watches, but that isn't right either. Whoever you are, I will pass on the warning I got. Intelligence is dangerous. I suspect human decency is too. Be careful."

Her heart skipped a beat when he mentioned watchers, but he said she wasn't one. *What was he talking about? Who was dangerous? Why did he warn her?*

She wrestled with her thoughts until they got to the ground and jumped off. Katerin caught and steadied him when he almost lost his balance. When he was steady on his feet, she turned to see Vassily staring at her with loathing. His gaze travelled to the crutch and his mouth twisted cruelly. Katerin put her hand on it and reinforced its being. *Be straight and steady, resist.*

Vassily frowned, then glowered at her and made a subtle sign with his hand. She'd seen one of her seniors do something similar when meeting a boy in the green. Katerin copied what she'd seen. Vassily paled, then nodded and ignored her.

Frederick led her to the exit and back into the courtyard.

"Vassily tried to warp my crutch, but he couldn't." Frederick glanced at her. "What did you do?"

"Maybe he couldn't work from that distance, manipulating wood is hard."

"Vassily could make my crutch dance from that distance, he's done it before. Yet something stopped him. I've never heard of anything which could stop aetheric influence."

"Didn't you say that intelligence is dangerous?" Katerin said. "Curiousity is too."

"Really?" Frederick turned away. "I'm coming to think that being alive is dangerous for me, but living is the only revenge I have." He sounded like when he'd told her to stay away, harsh and cold. "I think I saw food booths over in that direction." Frederick pointed, his voice reverting to the neutral tones he'd used to describe the clockworks.

"I am a little hungry, as long as there are no springs in my food." Katerin gave thanks for the sudden shift in mood.

"I will ensure you will not be eating clockwork." Frederick grinned at her, as if the cold, angry person was another person entirely.

Chapter 6 A Clockwork World

Frederick watched Katerin laugh; he'd not expected the food to be anything but normal, but the circus people created simple clockworks with pretzels and taffy. When she'd finish laughing Katerin convinced Frederick to buy her a monkey which made a face at her.

"I can't eat it." Katerin handed it to Frederick. "It feels too alive."

"I would never have imagined this." He turned it around in his hand, seeing how it worked. For the first time he paid attention to how he knew. If he closed his eyes a schematic appeared telling him what changes he could make. As an experiment he moved one of the taffy strands and the monkey's face changed.

He snapped the strands and handed it back to Katerin.

"It is safe now."

Katerin pulled a pretzel cog off and nibbled on it. Frederick bought a different clockwork snack and played with the movements until the taffy gave out.

They bought bread and cheese which didn't move and wandered through the circus. Men and women in red called out to the crowd promising clockwork wonders, next show in half a bell. The one they went to, featured a show with simulacrum performing a play. Most only had one spring, but the main characters had to have had more than three, or they had different clockworks for parts of the play.

The story was simple enough: a young farmer leaves home looking for his fortune. He runs into undesirable characters, one who tries to control his mind, another who attempts to control his body. The boy defeats both with a combination of wit and skill at clockwork building.

The final scene had him going underground where he met a people who never show a clear shape. One tells him to go to the city, build a clockwork dog to chase its tail and sit by the fountain.

He does and meets a girl who falls in love with the dog, and then him. Her father requires him to build ever more complicated figures.

"Have you ever heard stories of the underground people?" Katerin asked him when they returned to the sunlight path of the circus.

"I don't recall living with anyone who told me stories." Frederick said. He winced at the sharpness of his words. "My mother died when I was young. I have no memories of her at all. My father left not long after, and any recollection I have of him is blurred. I have lived with my guardian as long as I can truly remember. There was a woman when I was younger, but when I turned twelve, she was dismissed."

"She didn't tell you any stories at night?"

"The only thing she told me was to behave and eat my greens."

"I grew up with stories." Katerin looked down, maybe to hide watery eyes. "The things my ancestors strived for, my place in that struggle, but also tales like the one we just saw, meant only to entertain."

"Did you hear stories of these underground people then?"

"One of my friends mentioned her gran telling her stories of them, but apparently she went mad."

Frederick shivered as a chill ran up his back.

"What's wrong?" Katerin turned her concerned eyes on him. He was familiar with them from all the times she'd crouched beside him to heal and help, but something in him said there was more to them than he could remember.

"I know about losing people, but I would imagine having someone you love go mad to be a horrendous experience."

"You are right." They wander through the area, listening to the people in red calling out for their shows, but not going to see any. Frederick had a feeling Katerin needed time to think, so he kept silent unless she asked about something.

"Come see the most complicated clockwork ever made." The caller waved at the passing crowd. "It will tell your fortune from your writing on a card."

Katerin brightened and pulled Frederick into the line.

"You must look at it and tell me all about how it works."

"If it is as they say, I won't understand it any more than you." Frederick didn't want to see the thing. He didn't know why, but the idea of such a clockwork repulsed him. Yet for Katerin's sake he'd suffer through the experience.

They shuffled forward until they were close enough for a young woman in blue holding a basket to hand them a card and a pencil for them to sign. She took the pencils back but told them to hold on to the card.

"She is the youngest person we've yet seen working here." Katerin glanced back at the girl. "I don't think she's even my age."

"Maybe they keep the younger ones hidden from the crowd. They are builders, in a city where builders are loathed. I would not wish my children to experience that."

"You plan on children?" Katerin nudged him, as she did when she teased.

"Honestly, I don't even plan on surviving my years at the academy, but if I come out with no worse scars than I have, it would be nice to have someone to share my craft."

"That does sound nice." Katerin fiddled with her card.

"What about you?" Frederick asked.

"I must." Katerin blushed, "I mean, I would be happy to have children."

A young man, also in blue, pulled the door of the tent aside.

"Put your card, with the signature face up, in the slot. Then walk to the other end and it will return your card with your fortune on it."

"What would happen if we wrote a false name on the card?" Frederick looked at his name scratched in blocky letters.

"The clockwork doesn't care. It isn't the name, but the hand writing it." The young man waved them in.

"He sounded like he gets asked that question a lot." Katerin frowned back at him.

"Or a variant, perhaps people ask if they can't write their names, or if they seek fortunes for their children."

"You're right." Katerin stepped to the slot marked by a large arrow in case they missed it. She slid her card in.

Frederick didn't recognize the script on the card. He'd already guessed she wasn't what she claimed, but he had no clues to who she was. Maybe now he had one. He pushed his card into the clockwork, then they walked along the length of it. About halfway along it, he chuckled.

"What's so funny?" Katerin glanced at him.

"The clockwork is complicated indeed, but not because it has an unusual number of springs or actions. It is many clockworks hooked together, one winding the next as it performs another action. No single work has over two springs, but all of them together?" Frederick shrugged. "I've lost count of them, and the way they are put together, I can only get a glimpse of the intended purpose of it. It is a truly ingenious clockwork and one I wished I'd thought of myself."

"So each part does one thing?" Katerin scratched her head. "Let's count to see if our fortunes have the same number of letters."

"I think you are right." Frederick said.

They arrived at the end and the card popped out in the order they were placed in. They'd seen people in front pick theirs out and flip them over. Frederick only glimpsed that strange writing before she flipped hers over and paled.

"What is it?" He took his, but shoved it in his pocket without looking at it.

"Nothing, it's just the words struck a chord in me." She handed him her card. "I'd rather not talk about it."

To fill a parent's shoes, one may need an enemy more than a friend.

"That is strange." Frederick handed it back. "But I am more surprised it makes any sense at all."

They walked past couples eagerly comparing their cards. The words had been sharp and clear, not written by hand. He'd heard of clockworks which could draw simple pictures. Words would not be harder. It was putting them together in a way that had meaning which confused him.

The sight ahead put all thought of the cards out of his mind. An enormous tent towered over them. He guessed it had been on his side of the cage, and so they hadn't seen it from far above.

"Everything you've seen has been the barest introduction of what you will witness here." The man calling to the crowds wore the silvery coat and top hat of the poster.

There was no one in red collecting money, so the mob poured in and snagged whatever space they could on the simple benches.

Frederick found them two spaces near the front on the far side. An aetheric boy with a girl on his arm glared at them, but Katerin stared them down.

"He's about half rank in my class, probably furious that he couldn't push me around, but more scared that you are with me. That won't fit in his tiny brain."

"That's the second time you've talked about the aetheric being stupid." Katerin frowned at him. "Where do you get that idea?"

Frederick glanced around, but all those near him were occupied with each other or bouncing in anticipation of the show.

"I don't know what they teach at your school, but this term we have three classes. The first is why aetherics should have their power, the second is how to use it. The third is how it works. Guess which class the students complain about?"

Katerin wrinkled her forehead, but they dimmed the lanterns before she could speak, and a single beam illuminated the center of the ring.

The man in the silvery coat and top hat stepped into the light. The crowd gasped. He now had gears covering half his face, as if he himself were part clockwork. Frederick's breathing quickened at the sight.

"Ladies and Gentlemen, welcome to the Clockwork Circus. We travel the world to bring you the strange, the magical, the terrifying. Sit back and watch. Please don't interfere with the clockworks, at our last show we had someone who wanted to show off to his girlfriend. They were still picking pieces of copper and brass out of people when we left. If you wish to try destroying one of our clockworks, we have an arena where you may try your luck in relative safety." He lifted his hands. "Now I present to you—the Clockwork Circus." The beam of light vanished, and another appeared high above them. A wire ran from one pole to another, on top of the pole was a huge clockwork, but instead of springs to run it a man crouched in the centre. He stood, and Frederick had to look twice to be sure he was seeing right. The man stood in encased in a large man-shaped simulacrum.

"I present Skattigrim. He not only runs the clockwork; but will walk the machine across that thin thread of wire. Be silent, this takes the utmost in concentration."

Skattigrim moved levers, and the simulacrum waved to the crowd. It then stepped out onto that wire and Frederick held his breath along with everyone else. The thing wobbled, moving this way and that, always a hair's width from disaster. When it had almost reached the far post, its foot missed the wire and, in an effort to regain balance, Skattigrim made the machine roll backwards along the wire. A fall was inevitable. Screams came from several directions, and general moan from all around.

The simulacrum didn't fall, instead it ended up balanced on one arm, absolutely still for a long second, then it flipped to land rock steady on the wire where it had wobbled precariously only minutes before. It performed an impossible set of acrobatic stunts. Frederick watched transfixed. He'd never imagined such a thing before.

The act ended with the clockwork acrobat apparently missing the wire on a backflip. Again, screams and groans rose from the audience, but Frederick grinned. The thing's hand caught the wire, then as if it was melting, the clockwork unfolded around Skattigrim until he stepped lightly to the ground and bowed to the audience. Cheers and whistles deafened Frederick, and he joined in, perhaps for a different reason. He'd seen an entirely new realm of possibility for his art. Already his mind filled with schematics.

The light on Skattigrim vanished and shone on the far side of the ring where a troop of immense clockwork animals marched into the ring. The show continued unabated for a full bell before the single beam illuminated the Clockwork Man, as Frederick thought of him.

"I am sad to announce that our show has concluded, I hope you enjoyed what you saw." The answering 'yes' came as a roar. Then the beam went out leaving the tent in darkness for an instant before the rest of the lanterns came on. Ushers in red uniforms organized the crowd's exit even as the people for the next show began trickling in the other side.

"I have never seen anything like it." Katerin bounced on her toes in excitement.

"Nor have I." Frederick stretched until his joints popped and she had to steady him before he lost his balance.

They wandered through the maze on the far side of the tent. There were games of luck and skill, though Frederick didn't there was much luck involved. Enough people won tiny clockworks to keep the crowd gathering around spending their money.

As promised an arena held a selection of clockworks. Aetherics were challenged to destroy one. The materials in the arena might have looked like lumber, but Frederick suspected they were alive. Mityri's friends gathered around him cheering as a slender golem dismantled the clockwork, purpose-built to fall into reusable gears and springs. They awarded him with an exquisite dancer, which he accepted gracefully, then passed to the aetheric girl beside him.

Katerin tried a few of the games but had little luck. They moved past the games to booths selling all manner of things, some even finer than those at the beginning.

"I would love to buy something." Katerin turned in a circle. "But I have no idea what to get."

"Allow me." Frederick peered at each booth, then led her to one with a smaller crowd around it. Where the others had dancers or animals, this booth held flowers which grew from bud to bloom and back to bud.

"This is the finest work here." Frederick dug into his pocket and pulled out his coins. "Pick one."

"I couldn't they must be—"

"Pick one." Frederick interrupted her. "Today we are Frederick and Katerin, you said it yourself. I wish to do this for you."

"Very well." Katerin pointed at a flower which began as a midnight black bud but unfolded into bright gold.

"You have a discerning eye." The man behind the counter wore a grey uniform and was older than any other they'd seen. Frederick paid, though it took his last coin. Katerin held it like it was made of the finest gold, not coloured brass.

They walked through the gates and Frederick had to shake himself to return to the world of builder and aetheric.

"Thank you for a most marvelous day." Katerin's face glowed pink. She leaned over and brushed her lips against his cheek. "Whatever separates us, let us try to be friends."

Frederick put his hand up against his face as she walked away, still examining her flower.

Chapter 7 Blood and Bone

Frederick arrived at his rooms and went straight down to his workshop. He hauled his project to the table and stood back to look at it. Brass plates formed a skin around clockworks which were to work the heavy joint where his knee once was, others managed the ankle. He'd tried to wear it but couldn't take more than a step before falling. He might as well have made the thing from lead.

First, he stripped off the skin - useless weight -he didn't need it to look like a leg. The skeleton of steel he left alone, as well as the leather cuff to attach it to the stump of his left leg, but the rest he stripped out, carefully placing the parts away where he could find them again.

"I need something to replace the taffy." Frederick couldn't come up with any ideas, no steel coil spring in his workshop was strong enough.

He used a pencil to wind heavy brass wire then tried drawing it out. It stretched easily enough but had almost no return. Copper wire didn't work any better. It needed something stronger yet. It would have to be steel, yet the steel either refused to bend, or cracked. He'd have to visit the smith. *Do I have enough money?* Frederick set that aside for the moment and went back to assessing the clockwork leg.

The foot needed to move more naturally, bending only at the ankle would lift him up and take more effort to move and balance. Frederick took his shoe and sock off and examined his foot. It could rotate somewhat on the ankle, but by the toes, another joint simply bent and straightened. He walked with his crutch, trying to move his foot as if he had two good legs. That second joint was shock absorption, then it released the energy to help with the step. He hardly needed clockwork, only a strong spring, but a mechanism would let him control the power of the spring, and maybe take excess energy to wind another spring where the ankle was. He could do the same thing at the knee and be able to adjust for walk and running. In fact, he'd have to be careful he didn't overbalance his good leg with the new one.

Frederick did not know how long he worked before Granfle stomped downstairs.

"You missed school." The man glared at Frederick. "It is forbidden for an academy student to forgo attendance."

"I don't belong at that place."

"That is for the Warden to decide." Granfle tugged at his collar. "He expects you to attend and will take no excuses."

"What does he care?" Frederick stretched, working out kinks and pains from his concentrated effort.

"He cares, I don't know why. He doesn't confide in such as me." Granfle turned and headed for the steps.

"What did he say to get you to come down here?" Frederick asked.

"His messenger informed me you were to be in school tomorrow. If you happened to die between now and then, I was to send you in your coffin and prop you up in place. If I failed, the coffin would be mine. So, if you are not out the door in time for school, I will have everything in this clutter melted down and sold for scrap."

"I will not let you down, Sar Guardian."

"Do not mock me, boy. I didn't choose this role, but I will enforce its conditions. The main one being that you attend the academy."

"And what are the other conditions?" Frederick's hand tightened on a brass cog.

"I will tell you when you need to know them." Granfle heaved himself up the stairs.

Frederick looked around at his work, then sighed, until he could find another place to experiment, he was dependent on Granfle. He headed upstairs to shower and lay out his clothes for school.

***

"LeSille, so glad you deigned to rejoin us. You will report to the Warden at lunch for your punishment." Professeur dove into his lecture without another word to Frederick. Vassily strolled in barely in time to leave again.

The time in the back field making golems ended up as a game of tag with the student's golems chasing Frederick, students whose creations landed blows gained points and would move toward the front. It was impossible from the beginning, so Frederick concentrated on keeping Vassily's golem at bay. Other golems would disintegrate at a blow from his crutch, even an unintended one. But Vassily's would climb to its feet with its fixed grimace. Occasionally the crutch twisted in Frederick's hands, but the golem would slow in its advance.

Frederick's clothes hung in tatters by the conclusion of the class. Vassily's golem had landed powerful blows on Frederick, but not to knock him down. Frederick clubbed the golem to the ground, then pinned it with the end of his crutch until something snapped inside it and the thing ceased moving.

The students left Frederick behind as he wearily hopped toward the Warden's office. Of course, it was a room at the top of the tallest tower. He leaned against the wall to regain his breath.

"Don't keep me waiting, LeSille." The Warden's voice came deep and strong through the oak door which opened as the man spoke. Frederick hopped through and stood at the center of a plush carpet.

With luck, he'd bleed on it and ruin it. "While you are at this school, I am the absolute authority."

The Warden sat behind a large desk. Frederick expected someone older, or perhaps softer, but this man looked like he could snap any student in half without breaking a sweat. A sword hung on the wall behind him. The grip was well worn. A statement: *I'm dangerous, be afraid.*

Frederick met the Warden's gaze and didn't speak.

"Are you mute, boy, what do you have to say for yourself?"

"I didn't choose to attend this place; I didn't agree to its rules. Yet here I am." Frederick waved a hand. "I'm sure you know why I'm here, and from the fuss being made, it is important. So why don't you punish me and stop wasting your time trying to intimidate me."

"I could order you to jump out that window and you would."

"No, Sar Warden, I would not. You could break your own law and force me, but that would not make me obedient."

The Warden scowled, standing and snatching the sword from the wall.

"Are you going to cut off my other leg? Maybe an arm? You think that will make me obedient?" Frederick glared at the man.

The sword whistled through the air to stop a hair's breadth from Frederick's throat.

"You will go downstairs and hand this to Vassily and tell him the Warden orders him to give you ten hard lashes." The sword moved to pick a lash from the wall and toss it at Frederick. "Consider this your second warning boy, despite what you think, you are not indispensable. Push us too hard and we will crush you until you beg to be allowed to leap from my window." The Warden returned to his seat and began cleaning his sword.

Frederick hopped down the stairs into the lunchroom. He went over to where Vassily sat laughing with his cronies.

"Your lucky day, Harnchev, the Warden orders you to give me ten hard lashes." The lash landed with a thump on Vassily's lunch.

Vassily growled, snatched the lash and struck Frederick across the face.

"One." Frederick said. The next blow struck the stump of his leg sending the memory of pain through him. "Two." The blows landed hard and fast. The room counted along with Frederick. At ten, a senior student caught the whip.

"You're done."

"I'll be done when I say I'm done." Vassily wrenched the whip from the student and slashed it across Frederick's face a second time, opening a cut on his forehead. He grinned at Vassily. "What are you grinning about, builder?"

"You've disobeyed the Warden in front of the entire school." Frederick hopped to the table to pick up Vassily's napkin and dabbed at the cut on his face.

Vassily looked at the lash in his hand, and his face paled.

"Go report to the Warden." The senior student pointed to the door. As Vassily walked out of the room his hands shaking, the senior student clubbed Frederick to the floor. "I should beat you within an inch of your life."

"That is your right, Sar Classman." Frederick looked up at him. "But you weren't holding onto that lash very hard, were you? How deep into this game do you want to go?"

The student kicked Frederick in the ribs and stalked out of the room.

***

Frederick lurched into his basement workroom and looked around. He had to find a better place, one where he wasn't being watched. Stupid to think Granfle didn't know what was going on in his own home.

He turned and forced himself up the stairs and out onto the street. Katerin put her hand over her mouth as he hopped over to her.

"What happened to you?" She brushed her fingers over his head and the pain receded.

"I displeased the Warden." Frederick winced as his ribs complained but grimaced through the pain. "I don't know what game they are playing with my life, but I tire of it."

"Do you deliberately set out to anger them?" Katerin laid a hand on his rib and the stabbing sensation retreated.

"Yes." Frederick scowled. "How else will I learn from them? Like most people they are stupid when they are angry."

"And you, are you a fool when angered?" Katerin stepped back to stare at him.

"More than most." Frederick shook his head. "I need a place to work which is not under their watch."

"I just happened by because I heard rumours."

"I know you're watching me." Frederick held up his hand. "You aren't with them, for now that is enough."

"Don't you care?" Katerin's hands clenched.

"You have done me nothing but good. Your secrets will wait." Frederick dropped his hand. "I can't be angry at you."

"I know a place where you may work in peace." Katerin turned and walked away. Frederick hopped after her. She led him through increasingly small streets to a building with one wall collapsed into rubble.

"The rest is solid; it will not fall on you."

"How do you know that?"

"How do you build your clockworks?" Katerin spun to leave but stopped at the mouth of the alley. "I didn't get to tell you how much I enjoyed the circus in your company." She disappeared into the shadows.

Frederick took the rest of the week to transfer his tools and metal to his new shop. It felt odd to work with one wall open to the world, but he never saw a single person the entire time.

He hung his work clothes in a corner out of sight and heard a rustle. The fortune he'd never looked at. Frederick pulled it out of the pocket and turned the crumped card over as he straightened it out.

An enemy with honour is better than a disreputable friend. Under it, written in pencil was another message. *Come alone.*

Tomorrow was a rest day. He'd planned to spend it in his new shop, but the message intrigued him.

In the morning, Frederick left his rooms early and went to his workshop to put on his other clothes. He didn't want to look like he belonged with those from the academy. When he checked to be sure the card was still in his pocket and the message was actually

there and not something he'd imagined, he found a silver coin. Was it there when he found the card?

Frederick shrugged and headed toward the circus.

Chapter 8 Copper and Brass

Entering the circus on his own was a different experience. With Katerin he saw things through her eyes and noticed details he could comment on. This time, what hit him was the noise. The clattering of clockworks, the screaming of children and their parents trying to restrain them.

How did we hold a conversation in all this? Frederick moved away from the gates and left some of the racket behind. Callers interrupted his thoughts, but he arrived at the tent with the fortune telling clockwork without realizing. This was as good a place as any to start the search for whoever wrote on his card.

When he was handed the card, he scratched 'The Builder' in harsh letters on the thick paper and handed the pencil back. Young men stood in line expounding on how the clockwork would work and how it could tell a fortune from graphite on paper. Frederick snorted, they weren't from his school, and they at least showed some imagination if not knowledge. He amused himself by picking apart their theories as they moved forward.

He did not know of a clockwork being able to read, couldn't imagine what would be needed to make that happen. There was a possibility of an aura transferring to the card. After all, the aetheric worked with something which might be called an aura. Yet how to get a clockwork to recognize it? Clockworks performed actions. They didn't consider what happened around them. A dancing doll would try to dance on sand the same as stone. That was a large part of the difficulty of creating them, trying to work around things out of the builder's control.

One older boy, probably a senior at his school insisted the entire process was random and had no meaning. Frederick agreed about the lack of meaning, but random? How did they make sure the messages made even the vaguest sense?

The boy in blue nudged Frederick.

"Pardon, Sar, but it is your turn."

"Thank you." Frederick stepped through into the gloom, flustered at being addressed with respect. No matter, time to put his card in and test if it read the same as the first.

He wandered along the clockwork paying more attention to the individual actions of the clockwork, catching glimpses of what he guessed was his card. Sometimes it was near to him, other times lost behind gears and springs. The thing made a strange noise. Frederick tried to filter out what he'd expect to hear from a clockwork. The rasp of gears, the singing of springs changing in tension. The arms the works drove clattered, but behind it all was a steady tapping.

If he was to make a clockwork write, how would he put the words on the paper? Printing press made the most sense. A word or letter placed one at a time. Each work would handle one part of the sentence.

"Aren't you going to take your fortune?" A young girl behind him pointed at the card poking out from the slot.

"Yes, thank you, I was just entranced by the clockwork." Frederick plucked his fortune out and slipped it into his pocket.

"It is just a thing. It can no more think for itself than a rock." She snatched hers out, and eagerly turned it over. "Bah, it's nonsense." Tossing the card aside, she stalked out of the tent. Frederick picked up the card and looked at what had caused such disgust in her.

'The one in front is behind you.' It made little sense. He shoved it into his pocket with his and wandered out into the sun. A place of relative quiet would help him think. The great circle he and Katerin had ridden.

The line wasn't nearly as long as for the other machines.

"This is better at night. You can see lights all over the city." The boy in front of him tried to take the girl's hand, but she slipped it out of his reach.

"Behave, or you'll ride it alone."

"They won't let you ride it alone. Two to a cage." He tried again to capture her hand, and she walked off in a huff. The boy moved to follow her.

"Don't." Frederick put his hand up. "Let her think you'll not change her mind by force."

"What will change it then?" The boy sneered at Frederick. "You are as alone as I am."

"No, I'm alone by choice, and don't mind my own company."

"Idiot." The boy ran off through the crowd and Frederick put him out of his mind.

"Harvid, another single." The man taking the coins waved to one standing to the side. A woman stood with him. "Go over there, Harvid will put you in the cage with her, don't worry, she likely don't bite."

"Thank you." Frederick waved his crutch. "I wouldn't taste that good anyway."

The man laughed, and Frederick walked over to join Harvid and the woman. She might have been an age with the Professeur.

"You will put me in a cage with a builder?" The woman stared down her nose at Frederick's feet.

"That or you wait longer." Harvid shrugged. "Don't care which."

"Don't touch me." She pointed into Frederick's face.

"I will give you the utmost respect, Feren." Frederick bowed, carefully keeping his distance. The woman sniffed and followed him and Harvid to a cage. Frederick stood back to allow the woman on first, then hopped into the cage, deliberately putting the crutch between them.

They bobbed and rocked up to near the top when the thing lurched and stopped. Frederick looked down to see a man in blue arguing with the men in grey at the capstan.

"We may be here a while, Feren."

"Why do you say that?" She sniffed but looked at him with a little interest.

"The men who wind the spring are upset. I'm guessing it is off balance somehow and needs adjusting before they can wind it. It happens occasionally."

"How long before they fix it?"

"A man has run off, I expect to bring a builder to do the work." Frederick wished they were lower to the ground, and he could see better.

"Hmmph." She dug into her purse, pulled out a tattered book and a pencil. "Where was I?" Running the pencil down the page, she muttered to herself. "Ha." The line where she stopped had blank spaces, as did the ones below it. Above she had penciled words into the spaces.

"My deepest pardon, Feren, but what kind of puzzle is that? I've never seen the like."

"It isn't so much a puzzle as a test of imagination." She spoke with the enthusiasm of a devotee. "See there these words in the book, they frame the space. The trick is to put a word in the space to make the sentence work. A good player can use the lines to write an entire story."

"And you are a good player?"

The woman became a little pinker. "Better than some." She wrote a word into a space and ignored Frederick.

He pulled out the cards and looked at them.

'The one in front is behind you.' The girl's card was nonsense

'*To gain revenge, walk straight.*' His card didn't make much sense either. There were fewer words than the cards he and Katerin got back the first visit. Maybe the clockwork needed adjusting. The most complicated clockwork in the world probably needed the most fussing. If the thing was missing words, it wouldn't make as much sense. He glanced over at the woman's page. The framing words held the sentence together. If they weren't there, then the words would be like mismatched cogs. The workings came together in his mind. He laughed in delight.

"What is so funny?" The woman peered at him.

"I just figured out something. It was much simpler than I expected."

"Things often are. Unnecessary complication is the bane of a well-lived life."

"You are right, Feren. I feel most fortunate to have been your companion." The cage swung wildly, but the woman hardly flinched, just tucking the book and pencil away.

"It seems we are once again under way." The movement smoothed out and cheering came from some cages, and boos from others.

"How did you lose your leg?" The woman glanced at him from the corner of her eyes.

"It fell off, Feren." The usual line flowed off his lips. "I expect it will return someday to tell me of its adventures."

"Most amusing, builder, and a good way of deflecting pity." The woman nodded.

They arrived at the bottom. Harvid opened the door. Frederick hopped out, tangled his crutch, and fell hard to the wooden deck. Harvid ignored him to help the woman off.

"Please move on, the next cage is coming."

Frederick pushed himself up and gave himself a shake and caught the woman staring at him.

"It must be hard to have been abandoned by a part of yourself."

"I must admit it is a trial," Frederick said, "but better a leg than a heart." He bowed again and hopped away.

"You need to learn to fall, boy." A man who looked somewhat familiar stepped up beside Frederick.

"Are you going to teach me?" Frederick rolled the shoulder he'd jarred when he hit the ground.

"I could if you wish. I have a bit of time before the next show."

"Skattigrim." Frederick stopped and looked openmouthed at the man.

"Not so loud, or we'll be mobbed for sure." Skattigrim point to the side. "We'll find a little quiet over there."

The walked between two tents that Frederick would have sworn had no space between them. On the other side was a space bordered by fabric on all sides. In the center, a wooden floor rose above the cobbles.

"Climb up here, boy. Watch your footing, it moves more than you're used to."

Frederick gingerly hopped up on the wood, and it sank under his weight. He bounced on his toes using the crutch to balance.

"Gives you a bit of spring; but would absorb some too."

"Smart boy."

"I'm a builder, knowing what things do is second nature to me."

"Builder, are you? Don't think I'll go soft on you for that."

Frederick laughed and lost his balance. He hopped trying to regain it, but ended up face down on the wood, still laughing.

"What's the joke, boy?"

"First time I heard someone suggest being a builder would make my life easier."

"Huh, you folks in Lexburgh are stranger than most." Skattigrim hoisted Frederick to his feet. "Now the trick to falling is to not stop moving. You hit flat, you hit hard." He demonstrated by falling backward on the floor, hitting with such a thump it lifted Frederick into the air briefly. Skattigrim bounced up. "The idea is to roll and redirect the force." He fell backward again, but he curled and rolled coming easily to a relaxed standing position.

"Your turn."

Frederick closed his eyes and pushed his crutch away. He fell back; but stiffened and hit hard.

"Blast." Another try resulted in the same result. "I'm going about this wrong. Think about rolling, not falling." This time he relaxed his leg and curved his back. The landing wasn't near as graceful as Skattigrim, but he rolled to the side instead of slamming into the floor.

"That's the idea. Keep working on it. I must dress for the show." Skattigrim pointed to a corner. "Go through there to get back out, but don't be obvious about it."

Frederick tried falling forward, backward, sideways. He collected a new lot of bruises but rolled more times than not.

"What are you doing?" A girl who looked a few years younger than him had her hands on her hips. "Rubes aren't allowed back here." The sun sparkled on her skintight outfit.

"Skattigrim was teaching me how to fall."

"Oh him." The girl rolled her eyes. "He's always bringing in strays." She pointed to his missing leg. "Let me guess you, did a very public face plant."

"Got it in one." Frederick grinned and rolled his shoulders. "I'm a lot more bruised now than I was then."

"Let me see you then." She waved her hand.

"Don't laugh too hard." Frederick fell back, collapsing and rolling. He pushed himself to his feet.

"Not bad for a beginner." The girl flipped up onto the floor and it hardly moved at all. "You got the right notion. But you need to push off with your legs, er leg," Her face reddened briefly, "to roll to your feet." She demonstrated, again barely disturbing the floor. The girl had a bewildering number of ways to fall and come to her feet.

"I'm a builder," Frederick protested, "brass and copper, not rubber like you appear to be."

"A builder!" She clapped her hands. "Wait here."

Frederick watched her bolt through the same corner Skattigrim had vanished into. He tried to fall like she'd said.

"You had better have a good reason for being here." A man who wouldn't come up to Frederick's waist stomped over and rolled onto the floor coming to his feet.

"Does everyone here roll around like a ball?" Frederick asked. The man charged Frederick and with a twist sent him sailing across the floor. Frederick curled into a ball and landed on his shoulder and rolled several times before stopping on his back. He sat up, then stood. "What—"

The little man sent him soaring again. Frederick rolled and came to his feet again. The man came at him and Frederick rolled backward to stay out of his way. He almost got to vertical before losing his balance.

"Careful, kid." The little man shouted at Frederick, but too late. The next hop took him off the wood floor. He dropped hard on the cobbles and his leg twisted. The choice was hurting the only leg he had or adding more bruises. Frederick kicked his leg out straight to keep it from spraining, but that made him land like a stone.

"Svad." A girl's voice floated into the darkness. "Did you throw him off the pad?"

"It was an accident Lylphy, really."

Svad must be the little man, so Lylphy is the girl. Frederick was proud of his deduction. He opened his eyes and tried to sit up.

"Oh, no you don't, not til Butcher's seen you." Lylphy held him down. "You took a good whack to the head." She glared at Svad.

A tall man in a black dressing gown wandered into the square.

"You sent Kander to get me, said someone was hurt." He peered at Frederick. "Where's his leg?"

"Wandering about having more fun than me." Frederick tried to sit up again.

"Not his leg, Butcher, his head."

"His head looks well attached."

"He fell on the stones and knocked himself out good."

"Oh, very well." The man folded himself until he sat beside Frederick. "Try not to scream." He put his hands on either side of Frederick's head and squeezed. The sensation was like fingers moved around inside Frederick's head. He didn't know if he should be intrigued or sick. Butcher took his hands away before Frederick's stomach won the debate.

"He'll be fine." Butcher stood in the reverse sequence of his sitting, then walked back out of the square.

"Butcher's odd, but he's the best healer I know." Lylphy said and held out her hand. "How many fingers?"

"Aren't you supposed to ask that before he's healed?" Svad tilted his head.

"Four fingers." Frederick said. "Can I get up now?" He sat up before they could answer.

"Oh no. Taffi!" Lylphy jumped up and ran to where a heap of metal lay on the stones. "I'm sorry, I'm sorry." She poked at what Frederick could see was an ancient clockwork.

"May I see?" Frederick put out a hand.

"I don't know." Lylphy looked at Frederick. "Are you really a builder?"

"Yes." Frederick put a hand to his head. "I don't think Butcher stirred up my brains too badly."

Lylphy giggled and put the clockwork in his hands.

Taffi was the oldest clockwork Frederick had ever held. The parts were tarnished and many of them bent. More than few cogs were missing, and the spring looked like it had broken before Frederick was born. But she tugged at him in a way no other work had. It was like she wanted to move, and her enforced stillness pained her.

"Where was she made? I've never seen anything like her." Frederick turned her over in his hands.

"I don't know. She was my mother's, and before that my grandmother's, and before that her mother's and—"

"We get the picture, Lylphy." Svad sighed. "If you let her, she'll go on back forever."

"Not forever."

"It feels like it."

"If you want me to fix her, I'd have to take to my shop." Frederick peered deeper into the works.

"No, you can't." Lylphy snatched the clockwork from him and held it tight.

"OK, I guess I can bring some tools and parts here. I'll have to guess what I need." Frederick pushed himself upright, and the world spun around him.

"Whoa." Svad grabbed him around the waist with an astonishing strength. "Take it slow, kid."

"I think I'm all right now." Frederick tried hopping to pick up his cane and the little man had to catch him again.

"Lylphy, how about you put Taffi to bed and bring some food. The kid's going to need to sit a piece."

She ran off and returned with not just a plate holding a roll stuffed with meat and vegetables, but a man Frederick recognized as the Clockwork Man of the circus.

"Lylphy says Svad used your head to crack the cobblestones."

"It wasn't his fault." Frederick looked up at the man and winced. "I rolled away from him and tried to come to my feet, foot, and went off the edge of the floor."

"I see." The man shook his head. "People have a distressing habit of getting hurt around Svad."

The little man shrugged; but didn't deny it.

"Eat up, then Kander will make sure you arrive at your home in one piece. After that is your own affair."

"He's going to fix Taffi." Lylphy said.

"You're a builder then?"

"Yes." Frederick almost cringed but forced himself not to. These people were different. "I should be able to do something for Taffi. I'll bring what parts and tools I need tomorrow after I'm done with school."

"Very well. None of our builders will touch her. Say she's haunted."

"Don't know about that, but there is something about her." Frederick shrugged.

The Clockwork Man left, and the three of them ate.

Kander turned out to be a young man a bit older than Frederick. He never said a word the entire walk back to Frederick's rooms, but at the door he handed Frederick a slip of paper, then ran off toward the circus.

Chapter 9 Revelation of Power

Frederick coasted through the day at the academy, paying little attention to either words or bruises, though Lectura had a new golem which took even greater glee in smacking Frederick's leg.

When they were released from the afternoon lecture, Frederick headed toward his rooms. Vassily waited on the corner.

"Sorry, I have no time to play today." Frederick swung past. Vassily jumped forward and bumped Frederick. The roll came without thinking, as did the placement of the tip of his crutch between Vassily's legs. The other boy knelt groaning, holding himself as Frederick left him behind.

Frederick stopped at his rooms long enough to dump his books and change, then he was out the door. Halfway to his shop, he spotted Vassily following.

"Subtle." Frederick angled away from his shop the river which cut through Lexburgh to the west of the circus and Frederick's workshop.

Though the locals called it a river and there were bridges across it, there was more mud than water at this time of year. Frederick led Vassily over a bridge, then along a walkway beside the muck. The stink wasn't too bad. Frederick remembered it reeking horribly when he'd played here as a much younger boy.

The stones were still there, though Frederick paused as he considered his options. He'd never crossed the river with one leg. *No, not quite true. There was that dare.* It had resulted in him arriving home black with mud. Granfle had made him strip and wash at the water pump in the square.

He hoped the cause of him losing the dare was still as treacherous. Frederick glanced toward the bridge. Vassily made no attempt to hide. After making a point of looking in all directions, Frederick slipped down to the riverbed. He hopped onto the first one, then kept moving as fast as he dared, counting stones under his breath. At fifteen he skipped a stone, then again at nineteen, the last at twenty-three. A few more jumps and he climbed to the path on the other side of the river where he ran under a bridge. In the shadows he scrambled onto the roadway, then headed back toward his workshop. He hadn't gone far before a bellow of rage from the riverbed rewarded him. Vassily would be awhile pulling himself out of the mud.

Just in case, Frederick left the main road and took back streets to the alley leading to the falling down building. He paused deep in the shadows, but no one moved on the street.

In the shop, Frederick packed everything he thought he might need and then some. The bag dragged on his back and forced him to depend more on his crutch. When he was in sight of the circus gate, he remembered the slip of paper Kander gave him. It was a crude map showing him another entrance to the circus.

Kander opened a door; indistinguishable from the wall when closed and waved him in.

"Thanks." Frederick puffed. He stretched and waved Kander to lead on. This path had no noisy clockworks nor crowds. It led past wagons, some looked like houses on wheels, others were flat beds of wood. Frederick didn't see, or smell, any animals to pull them. Maybe they used the clockwork animals.

Past the wagons, they ducked into a narrow alley between tents. The sounds of the crowds filtered in from both sides. Kander pulled a tent door open and waved Frederick in. The cloth slapped into place behind him.

"Well, don't just stand there, boy. Come in to where I can see you." The voice came out of the gloom at the other end of the tent. Frederick moved in that direction, feeling ahead with his crutch.

"That's better."

"I still can't see a thing." Frederick blinked, but the gloom didn't lift.

"You have your eyes, boy, and I have mine." The voice was closer. It rasped as if the speaker wasn't quite human.

"You've grown, though not as tall as I'd hoped. How are you enjoying school?" The cackle which followed the question made Frederick shudder.

"If you are asking, you already know the answer."

"That I do, boy." The words came from Frederick's right this time. "They're watching you."

"So I've been warned." Frederick leaned on his crutch as the bag on his back grew heavier.

"Not those pitiful aetherics with their plots. The Phemerals, the source of real power."

"Phemerals?" Frederick shook his hand. "I haven't heard of them."

"Good thing too." The words were whispered in his ear. "People who hear of them disappear."

"Or go mad?"

"Isn't that just another way of disappearing?"

"I guess." Frederick shifted his bag on his shoulder. "My bag is heavy. What is it you want of me?"

"Can't a father want to see his son?" The voice cackled again. "Though there's little left of the father you remember."

"I hardly remember him at all." Frederick let his bag slip to the floor with a clank. "It will take more than a voice in the dark to convince me you are him."

"Wise, wise." The words were soft, almost inaudible. "We'll talk again, you and I."

Light filled the tent and Frederick's eyes watered.

"This way." Kander said.

Frederick hoisted his bag and followed.

"Don't talk much, do you?"

"No need." Kander didn't turn around.

"You work for that person in the tent?"

"Owner. He owns the circus."

"That's clear." Frederick wobbled and almost fell. Kander lifted the bag from his shoulder.

"He owns the circus. I am part of the circus." Kander strode away. "You will be too."

They entered the square with the raised floor before Frederick could frame a question. Kander dropped the bag on the floor, then left.

"Thank you, I guess." Frederick sat beside his bag and rolled his shoulders to relieve the ache. Then he opened his bag to ensure everything had survived Kander's rough treatment.

"There you are." Svad came into the square. He wore a bright red suit, which, while not skintight, showed the muscles beneath. "I'll teach you some wrestling moves while we wait for Lylphy. She's practicing."

"Skattigrim was the only person aside from the Clockwork Man I saw in the performance."

"Clockwork Man?" Svad raised an eyebrow. "Oh you mean Baelophile. Clockwork Man, wait til I tell him."

"He won't be angry, will he?"

"Probably." Svad ran and did a front flip onto the wooden floor. "Come on, I'll show you some moves."

Frederick sighed, and put his bag safely off the platform, then lay his crutch beside it. He rolled onto the floor and came up to balance on his single leg.

"You've been practicing." Svad grinned evilly.

"Ever since I lost it."

"Now, in wrestling, the trick is to keep your weight low. That's why we Palcans are all but impossible to beat."

"If no one can beat you, why would they try?" Frederick tried bending his leg, but the strain made him stand up again.

"Now there's the question." Svad crouched. "Most people think Palcans are just little people with no strength." He launched himself at Frederick, taking them both to the floor. "I let them think so, until it is too late." Svad rolled off Frederick, then heaved him up onto his foot.

He coached Frederick on how to hold his arms, and where to grapple his opponent. The names of different moves flew off his tongue in a bewildering stream, but strangely, Frederick laughed and enjoyed himself.

"Oh great, another one?" Lylphy wailed and threw her arms in the air dramatically. Svad turned to look at her, so Frederick lunged at the little man taking hold of one leg and lifting as he'd been told. Svad's arms wrapped around his waist and held Frederick mid-air, helplessly flailing for a grip.

"When we wrestle." Svad didn't sound at all like he was holding someone twice his size over his head. "It is important to land with style."

Frederick caught a glimpse of Lylphy wincing before Svad tossed him toward the center of the floor. He tucked his arm under him, so he landed and rolled off his shoulder and kept rolling until he'd slowed enough to try coming upright.

Lylphy clapped enthusiastically, while Svad chuckled.

"You're a natural. A bit more training and we could wrestle for the rubes and really gull them in."

"Rubes?" Frederick checked to make sure all his pieces were still attached.

"That's what we call the people who come to see the circus." Lylphy waved her hand grandly. "Gulling means we confuse them, so we can take their money."

"Like the games of chance." Frederick said. "Some people win, but most lose, and don't notice it doesn't match the odds, or rather, what they should be."

"Smart boy." Svad frowned at him.

"Not my problem. They should pay more attention."

The palcan relaxed and Lylphy laughed.

"I told you," she said. "Fresh meat."

"That's up to Owner." Svad crossed his arms stubbornly.

"Fine, we'll settle when Owner makes it official." Lylphy lifted Taffi out of her bag. "Here. Fix her."

"I will have to take her apart to put her together." Frederick hopped over to his bag then sat down. He took Taffi from the girl's hands and turned the clockwork over to examine her more closely.

"Hmm, pretty much as I thought. Needs a new mainspring and two of the subsprings are pretty much gone too. Some of the gears are bent." He chose a tool and began quickly taking the clockwork apart, laying out her pieces in careful order beside him. "That's the main workings. I'll get them going before I worry about the actions."

Frederick went through his parts, finding replacements which would fit well enough. He'd have to add a cog or two, but he had plenty. One of the pieces puzzled him. Attached to the mainspring was a crystal almost as big as the spring. Wires ran from it to other parts of the work, but they were too thin to cause any movement. He snipped them off where they wouldn't tangle in the mechanism. The remainder fell off the crystal, so he gathered up the pieces, before removing the fused mainspring and replacing it with one he'd built.

Light oil loosened up joints that hadn't moved in ages. Then he began to reassemble her. He didn't pay attention to the passing of time until he put the last piece back in place.

Frederick lifted his head to talk to Lylphy and saw a rapt audience, mostly children younger than Lylphy.

"School's out, and they mostly come here to play, away from the rubes." Lylphy said from beside him. "Watching you is almost as good."

"Right." Frederick raised a key in his hand, then handed it to Lylphy then pointed to a hole in Taffi's back. Put it in there. You'll need to wiggle it until it seats properly, then do ten turns to the right. No more than ten."

"What happens if I do too many?"

"The spring could bind, and she won't work."

Lylphy gingerly stuck the key into the clockwork and turned it, counting softly. When she'd reached ten, she retrieved it.

"It isn't working."

"Most clockworks have a safety mechanism to lock the works while the spring is wound." Frederick crossed his fingers. "Lift her right arm up to shoulder level. You'll feel it click."

"Then what?"

"Put her on the floor and see what she does." Frederick shrugged. "I can make a guess from the workings, but there are things I don't recognize."

"You do it." Lylphy pushed Taffi into his hands.

He balanced her on feet, holding the body, then pulled the arm up until it clicked. Something shocked his hand, and he yanked it away. A tiny red dot on his palm faded quickly.

Taffi whirred, and for a moment he thought nothing would happen, then she took a step forward, lifted her arms over her head and spun. Her left leg lifted behind her, then she bent forward from the waist until her leg and body were in a straight line. The spin stopped, and Frederick expected her to stop there, she'd only had two sub-springs, but she leaned forward until her hands hit the floor. With a loud click, the right foot pushed out making Taffi flip over her hands to land on her right foot, then bring her left into place. Her arms dropped slowly to her side.

The mob of children clapped and cheered, while Lylphy jumped up and down in excitement. She wound the clockwork again and set her into motion. Frederick didn't see her yank her hand back, so the thing didn't shock her. It went through its movements, smoother this time.

Lylphy put her through her paces a dozen times before she reluctantly put it back in her bag.

"Keep the key, it goes with the spring." Frederick stood and stretched. "I'm glad she works, I have to admit I was worried, as old as she is."

"You must come and eat with us and meet the others." Lylphy grabbed his hand and pulled him. Frederick had to hop frantically to keep up with her.

They wound between tents, the children giggling softly, barely audible over the noises of the circus. At a plain brown tent near the parked wagons, Lylphy pulled him inside and over to where a woman in a red uniform sat with a steaming cup in front of her.

"Mom, look. She works." Lylphy set Taffi on the table and wound the spring, then set her into action.

The woman watched the clockwork in silence, then clapped when the performance was over.

"And this must be the builder you have chattered about since yesterday."

"Frederick." He bowed slightly. "I'm happy to have been of some service."

Svad jogged into the tent, Frederick's crutch under his arm, his bag slung on his back.

"You left in such a hurry you forgot these."

Lylphy turned deep red and hid her face.

"It's okay, Lylphy, I knew they were safe."

"But I dragged you all the way here on one leg." She peeked out between her fingers. "I'm sorry."

"I go everywhere on one leg." Frederick grinned. "The crutch is only for balance when I need it."

"Like when getting off the great wheel." Skattigrim walked in, wearing his costume from his performance.

"Exactly so." Frederick's grin widened.

He sat with Lylphy and Svad while Skattigrim kissed Lylphy's mother on the cheek before taking his own seat beside her.

Children ran up with plates heaped with food and warm cup of a fragrant tea. They giggled at Frederick as he picked up the pair of thin sticks on the side of his plate.

"Like so." Lylphy demonstrated, then pushed his fingers into the proper place. Her hands were warm but didn't make him tingle like Katerin's. She made him feel like when he was a senior in the tiny school he'd attended with mostly builder children. Many of them looked up to him for some reason, and he'd enjoyed their company while not understanding it.

As the people in the tent finished their meal, the murmurs of conversation sounded around him.

"Papa, he fixed Taffi." Lylphy bounced her seat. She handed him the key. "Show him, Brass."

"Brass?" Frederick raised an eyebrow.

"You told me your name was Brass Ancopper."

Frederick roared with laughter, making Lylphy turn red again and attracting attention from the other tables.

"You're making fun of me." She pouted.

"Not at all," Frederick said. "It's a much better name than the one I have." He wound the spring and set Taffi in place. Again, when he lifted her arm, a shock hit his hand. Frederick held his hand in place this time and visualized what was there inside the clockwork. He moved away when her hands reached over her head.

"Why did you hold on to her so long?" Lylphy wrinkled her forehead. "Am I doing it wrong?"

"Not at all." Frederick handed her the key. "I was feeling what was going on inside her, making sure everything was running in balance." Taffi finished her routine. "She's working just fine."

Lylphy hugged him tight. "Thank you, thank you, thank you, Brass."

Frederick put an awkward arm around her shoulders. "Clockworks should work. It is what they are made for. I'm happy I could fix her."

"I'm surprised." Skattigrim picked the clockwork up and peered at her inside through the gaps in the plates covering her. "None of our builders would even touch her." He placed her back on the table.

"They grew up with too many old stories." Lylphy's mom's lips twitched. "In some tales, very old clockworks steal souls so they can become real people."

"I've never heard that." Frederick ran a finger across Taffi's head.

"Lexburgh is an odd place." Skattigrim shrugged. "There are aetheric and builders wherever we have been. They never exactly get along, but nowhere else is there the level of hatred seen here. I was reluctant to come after the last time, but Owner insisted. Said he had business here."

Me. Frederick's gut burned. Am I really his son? Did my father run away with the circus?

"Was last time about twelve years ago?" Frederick asked.

"That's right." Lylphy's mother said. "Lylphy had just learned to walk, and she kept escaping and running naked through the camp."

"Oh mom, really?" Lylphy's face turned pink.

"It's the truth." Her mom smiled.

"Because it is the truth doesn't always mean it needs to be said." Frederick spoke before he thought.

"I believe you are right, Brass." Lylphy's mom cupped her daughter's face. "My apologies, dear. I will try to find more appropriate ways of embarrassing you." Lylphy stuck her tongue out at her mom and her parents laughed.

Is this what it would have been like to grow up in a family instead of with a lawyer for a guardian?

Frederick's fist clenched under the table. He hadn't known just how much his father stole from him by running away.

The place Taffi shocked burned slightly on his hand. He took a deep breath and loosened his grip. Anger wouldn't bring back what he'd never had. With a smile he focused his attention Lylphy and her family.

Chapter 10 Dangerous Experiments

All week Frederick spent most of his free time at the circus. Once the word got around that he'd fixed Taffi and to all appearances, still had a soul, others asked for his help. He pushed the question of the shocks he'd got from the clockwork to the back of his mind.

"The blasted thing is a curse." Gears pointed at the fortune telling clockwork. "Breaks down more often than it works. I can work the big engines, they like me, but this thing?" He bared his teeth at it. "It hates me."

"Let me see what I can do." Frederick opened the case he had his tools and parts in. He'd found it covered with dust in a back room of the house he lived in. With a few changes it made a great tool carry.

The first part of the clockwork sent the cards on one of six different tracks, but if it was the slightest bit off, the tracks didn't get cards. The gears looked worn, so Frederick replaced them and adjusted the spring. After a few tests, the cards ran on all six tracks. The next bit on each track printed a few words. They were only a skeleton to hang the rest of the card's message on, but without them, the message wouldn't work. They were in better shape since they only handled a sixth the work as the first part. Each machine along the way added to the sentence. Either a fixed few words or a random word of more import.

Frederick worked his way along replacing cogs, tightening up the timing. There was one clockwork in the centre of the thing, he didn't understand. It didn't look to connect to any of the other elements, at least mechanically. It was much older than the rest, and like Taffi, had a crystal and those wires leading away. Here though, they broke off not far from the crystal.

He pulled the clockwork out of the machine and ran a test card. It worked perfectly without the old clockwork. He put it in his work bag so he could look at it in more detail in his workshop. That was assuming he ever spent time there again.

Life at the circus was as fulfilling as the academy was mind-numbing. Keeping in mind his discussion with the Warden. Frederick never missed class, though he spent his time at school wishing he was at the circus. The only effect was to make the time there drag interminably.

Vassily followed him every day, making the hairs on Frederick's neck rise, but the circus people had ways of dealing with rubes even outside the wall and Frederick made into the circus each day without Vassily seeing where he went.

The only downside of virtually living at the circus was he didn't see Katerin, except in glimpses out of the corner of his eye. They hadn't talked since she'd shown him to the abandoned house he used as his workshop when he wasn't at the Clockwork Circus.

"Hey, Gears," Frederick stuck his head into the maintenance wagon. "I think I have the blatherer working again. Tested good on a few cards. There was a weird thing stuck in the middle of it not connected to anything else. You mind if I poke around at it try to figure out what it did?"

"Heck no." Gears snorted and put his feet on his desk. "Anything to make that thing less complicated is an improvement in my eyes."

"Gears, mainspring on the wheel is out of alignment again." A man in grey shouted from the door, then vanished. "Gods preserve me, that this is almost as much trouble as the blatherer." He dropped his feet to the floor. "Come along, Brass. Maybe you can work your magic on the beast." They jumped to the ground and Frederick hoisted up his tool carry, while Gears carried a sack with tools and grease.

They made their way to the wheel and around to the building with the mainspring.

"The problem is we have to be able to move the blasted thing, so it isn't set up as tight as it should be. The spring wanders and it hits that." He pointed at a piece of wood. It looked like the capstan. "Last thing we want is the spring to break loose. It would wipe out the wheel."

"I've never seen anything like it." Frederick wandered in a circle around the spring. The metal, which should have been lined up flat, cupped upward toward the outside. He ran his hands along the metal. "You have some warp, about six coils in."

"Tell me something I don't know." Gears sighed. "The people who built this this live on the far side of the old kingdom. It would be a couple of months travel if we didn't stop along the way. Circus has to stop."

"Right, the show has to go on." Frederick said. He'd heard the mantra from everyone. "An aetheric could fix it, but I have no idea how to deal with it otherwise."

"Sure, Brass, you'll go out and ask, 'Pretty please, could you get your perfect hands dirty fixing out machine for us?'"

"I know one I can talk to." Frederick ran his hands along the coil again. "Just the one spot for now. Let me see what I can do."

"Now I know the real reason they call you Brass." Gears shook his head. "I'll believe it when I see it."

***

"I'm curious just what you aetheric's can do other than make golems wave sticks." Frederick came up beside Mitryi in the dining room.

"We can make golems wave swords. Bug me and I'll give you a demonstration."

"Too bad, I'd hoped aetheric manipulation might be more useful."

"Useful?" Mitryi frown at him. "We're aetherics, we rule Lexburgh."

"Being aetheric and useful is different from making use of aetheric manipulation to work with things."

"Why don't you ask the teachers?" Mitriyi stepped away.

"You know why that wouldn't be a good idea." Frederick spoke to his back, but the other boy stopped then turned to grab Frederick and drag him out of the dining room to the green. They walked until Mitryi was satisfied no one else was around.

"You are playing a very dangerous game, builder. They take their rules very seriously."

"You mean your rules."

Mitryi laughed, a bitter edge on it. He took a handful of Frederick's shirt and twisted.

"You aren't as smart as you think, and it is going to get you killed. I will watch and cheer."

"And in the meantime, play top of the heap in this place. I admit, not the best preparation for ruling the city."

"Are you *trying* to make me beat you?" Mitryi shook him.

"If I wanted a beating, I'd be taunting Vassily." Frederick kept his voice level. Mitryi pushed him down. Frederick rolled back to his foot a safer distance from the second year student.

"There's another who isn't as smart as he thinks." Mitryi shook his head in disgust. He fixed Frederick with a glare. "You aren't doing this for fun, so why don't you cut to the chase and save us both some time. Don't make the mistake of thinking I'm in any way less than your enemy."

"The mainspring on the big wheel at the circus is warped in one place. A small adjustment would put it to rights."

"And you expect me to do builder work?"

"No builder could do it." Frederick shook his head. "If we could, it would be fixed."

"Forget it." Mitryi walked past Frederick.

"I will tell them you are unable to do it."

Mitryi spun and punched Frederick in the eye, knocking him down, and this time he didn't roll. Pain shot through his head.

"Ok then." Frederick ground out words past his clenched teeth. "Ask for Gears at the wheel. He'll show you what needs to be done."

"What makes you think I'll do any such thing?"

"Pride." Frederick sat up, hand over his eye. "If you don't, you'll lie awake wondering." Blood trickled from his nose, turning his mouth to salt. Mitryi walked away without looking back. "You were right about one thing, Mitryi." He spat out blood. "None of us are as smart as we think."

***

Frederick's head ached, and his eye sent shooting pains through him. The noise of the circus would be too much. After school and changing clothes, Frederick headed toward his shop, keeping his customary eye out for Vassily.

"Don't worry, Vassily is not following today." Katerin stepped out of an alley and around to his right side where he could see her. She reached her hand toward his face.

"I earned this one." Frederick caught her hand.

"If I don't do something, you may never see out of that eye again." Katerin met his gaze with hers. "Your choice."

Frederick let go of her hand and she cupped it over his face.

"The bone of the cheek is broken and putting pressure on your eye."

"Mitryi throws quite the punch." Frederick winced as something moved under the skin of his face.

"Mitryi carries a roll of coin to add authority to his blows." Katerin answered absently, she stared into space as if her hand worked by touch.

"When Vassily worked aetheric on me, it was excruciating." Frederick's words slurred a bit as the left side of his face went numb.

"Vassily meant it to be as painful as possible, and he knows much less than he thinks."

"You're the second to say that."

"No, Mitryi said he wasn't as smart. That is also true."

"Of course you were there, you always are." Frederick refrained from shaking his head. "The owner of the circus talked about other watchers. Are you one of them?"

"The owner is twisted by what he's become as he searches for what can't be found."

"That's helpful." Frederick poked at his face carefully as Katerin dropped her hand.

"You're welcome."

"I meant your obscure comment about Owner. You sounded like a card from that clockwork."

"We thought the clockwork a joke, a toy. I think there is more to it. There was something in it which raised the hairs on my arms."

"You talk about it in the past tense. What changed?" Frederick tilted his head. "I fixed it just the other day."

"Whatever you did not only fixed it but changed some other fundamental." She caressed Frederick's face again. "Be careful at the circus, it isn't what it seems." Katerin stepped back into the alley and vanished in the shadows.

"Is anything?" He spoke to where she had stood. Free of pain he headed for his workshop. Suddenly he wanted to take a close look at what he'd removed from the fortune telling machine.

He moved the screen he'd made to hide his equipment, borrowing material and skill from his friends at the circus. They were some of the most straightforward people he'd met. Not that his circle of acquaintance approached anything normal. Maybe others in the city were like them

He lifted out the ancient clockwork and peered at it. The only way to learn would be to take it apart. It was a normal clockwork, in good shape for its age - better than Taffi. He set the pieces down in order. The spring with the crystal filled his cupped hand. It was much larger than the one in Taffy.

This one was more firmly attached to the spring. There was no place to insert a key. *What's the use of a spring I can't wind?* Sub-springs were wound by the action of the main spring. In some clockworks, that was its only purpose.

He put the mainspring with its crystal down and examined the clockwork to see if he'd missed places where sub-springs had once been mounted, perhaps to connect this work with the whole. The only connection came through the wires. Closer examination of the crystal revealed two colours of wire, brass and copper. Frederick took the ends of the wires and rolled them in his fingers.

Frederick woke on in complete darkness. *How did I get here?* The back of his head throbbed in time to the pain from his eye. It wasn't as bad as before

Katerin healed it, but something had unwound her healing. The only way that could happen is if she left some aetheric like a bandage to hold the pieces together.

Something had removed the bandage. A flash of brass and copper wires came into Frederick's mind. The clockwork? Was he still at his shop? If he was there should be the leg of his desk within reach. His fingers found it and he levered himself upright. He ran his hands gently across his desk but didn't find the mainspring.

I was holding it when I fell. He turned to orient himself. *It would have rolled this way.* Lowering himself to the floor he swung his hands in arcs, slowly moving forward. Something glowed faintly behind a brick on the far side of the building. He crawled to it and picked it up cautiously, using two fingers to avoid the wires. A rag hid the glow as he put it in his pocket. By guess he moved the boards covering the workshop.

Crutch in hand, Frederick felt his way to the alley, then out to the street. The faint light of a lantern beckoned. He hobbled from one pool of light to the next the rest of the way to his rooms.

***

Katerin watched Frederick enter his house. In the dark it had been easy to follow closely. She cursed herself for not telling him to go home, but she didn't want to explain how what she did was different than what an aetheric healer would do. He'd guessed she wasn't aetheric, but hadn't questioned her further, as if his only focus was the aetheric. Mitryi had understood Frederick's reference to "them". He'd hid it well, but even talking about them terrified him.

Out of curiousity, Katerin had gone to the circus after healing Frederick. Mitryi's work on the spring had been both powerful and subtle, leaving the circus people caught between fear and gratitude. Mitryi hadn't been invited behind the scenes.

She returned to check on Frederick and found him unconscious, near death. Katerin wasn't the slightest bit tempted to leave him to his fate. Frederick was the linchpin, somehow holding past and future together. When he began to stir, she'd fled to the deeper shadows to watch.

Only Frederick would worry about parts to a clockwork after coming near death.

***

At the academy, Frederick's vision in his left eye blurred, on and off through the day. Maybe he'd check with Katerin after school. He didn't see her on the way home, but thought it was going away on its own.

At his shop he pulled on a pair of thin leather gloves, then took out the mainspring and peered at it. The spring looked odd when examined through the crystal. Not distorted, clearer, as if he saw on a deeper level.

What had happened to him? He took endless precautions to stop from touching the two coloured wires. Pliers helped him wind them in tight springs. They contrasted oddly with the mainspring. He looked carefully and discovered steel.

Larger clockworks used steel, but it meant hiring a smith and hoping they created what was needed. The huge spring running the vertical wheel was steel, more than he'd ever seen in one place.

Frederick dug through the bag of parts he'd removed from old clockworks, sometimes he could reuse bits. He found the crystal from Taffi. It lay clear as water in his hand. The wires were gone, so he hadn't touched them. He heaved a sigh of relief. At least Lylphy wouldn't activate whatever strangeness had hit him last night.

"The other builders thought it was cursed. Clockworks were thought to steal souls." Frederick smacked his head, then regretted it. Throbs travelled down his neck. The crystal had taken something from him when he'd touched the wires. Aether that Katerin had left behind.

His hand trembled. If the crystals absorbed aether, he could make clockworks proof against aetheric taking them over. The more they tried the more it would charge the crystal. But he had no idea how the wires were connected to the crystal. They'd left no residue on the stone.

He pried it off the mainspring to examine it, then tossed the spring aside as useless. Holding it up to his eye revealed a world of painful sharpness. Stone had pinpoints of light. The wood table held tiny threads, disconnected from each other. When he looked at his hand it glowed, tiny beads of energy running along threads. Looking at the copper or brass he saw no light at all. The other crystal held a dense tangle of energy.

He found the magnifier he used for very tiny work. A bit of effort, and he had mounted the crystal so he could lower it over his left eye, since the blurriness didn't change how he saw the threads of aether.

Now what? He had a crystal which let him see aether. Did the aetherics see the world this way? Asking would give him away, but in none of the lectures, not even the afternoon one, was seeing aether mentioned.

The other crystal collected aether. He cautiously touched the wires to the stone, then the table, but nothing changed in his view through the crystal. It needed to be something living. It wasn't the soul clockwork stole, but the energy of life. Not that it would make a difference to the person. Eventually they would die.

Could he collect more? A plan formed in his mind. He picked up the pliers and set to work.

***

Frederick sat in his chair forcing himself to be still, no different than any other day. He couldn't risk gloves; they would be noted immediately. Thin pieces of leather separated his hands from the wires. He'd added wire from his own store, heavier, but it should do.

Horselli walked in and smirked at Frederick's still purple eye, then sat.

Frederick expected him to jump up and curse, which was why he held the wires beneath his desk ready to pull them away before Horselli saw them.

The other boy stiffened briefly, then slid boneless from his seat. Frederick pulled the wires back, wrapped them and the crystal and stuffed them inside his shirt. Then he shouted and jumped from his seat. He didn't need the crystal to know no aether ran through Horselli. Other students coming in ran over, then stopped as they saw Horselli lying on the floor.

"He just fell over." Frederick didn't need to fake the shake in his voice. One of the students bolted from the room, the others stared at Horselli.

By the time the Warden stalked into the room, followed by a white-faced student, a crowd had formed.

"He just fell over." Frederick's shaking grew as he contemplated the consequences of his experiment. It didn't matter that he hadn't intended to kill anyone.

The Warden knelt putting a hand on Horselli and frowned.

"He has no aether in him." He stood and glared down at the body. "It is rare, but if the aetheric ability is pushed too far, one can deplete the aether completely. I will have a word with Lectura about warning you students." He walked out of the class.

"What, what do we do with him?" A student pointed at the corpse.

"Carry him to the infirmary," Vassily spoke from the doorway. "They'll take care of shipping him home."

Four of them hoisted what remained of Horselli and carried him out of the room. After they returned Professeur walked in and began lecturing as if nothing had changed.

Chapter 11 Soul Stealer

Horselli's collapse was the subject of wild speculation. Especially the Warden's warning about overextending their aetheric ability. Frederick had his doubts, but the only way to check it out would require him to explain how he'd killed the boy.

The bundle of crystal and wire burned in his shirt. Guilt, fear, and elation fought for dominance in Frederick's thoughts. Lectura warned the boys using exactly the same words as the Warden, as if he'd memorized a script. After that the class proceeded as it always did, Vassily showing off, and the rest struggling with varying degrees of success to produce a golem which lasted more than a few seconds.

Vassily used his power to twist and manipulate objects without turning them into golems, surely that would be an easier first step.

He focused on the pile of stone while Lectura eyed him, then let his thoughts run when the man turned his attention elsewhere. The new golem had the same sadistic streak as the old one. Frederick gritted his teeth and ignored the thing. Then the golem started to climb up Frederick's leg, claws digging in for purchase. It reached toward where the crystal hid.

"Go over to Vassily and die." Frederick hissed, desperately hoping the first dissolution hadn't been an accident. The golem bared its teeth at him, but dropped from its perch and staggered toward Vassily. It bumped into other boys and slashed at their legs with its claws.

One student who tried to push it away ended up with a bite on his hand. His shout got the attention of Lectura who had been berating a boy opposite from Vassily. He looked up, his eyes went wide, and ran toward the creature. It reached Vassily before Lectura got close enough to touch it. For the second time, Lectura was left with a pile of rubble. He tried to recreate it but got only a twitch of a stone.

The boys whispered among themselves until Lectura shouted at them. He dismissed the class and loped toward the Warden's tower. The boys dashed off; whispers forgotten in the joy of extra free time. Even Vassily walked away without a backward glance.

If the golem was attracted to the crystal, the teachers might be able to spot it. Especially the third-class teacher. Frederick slipped into the vertical channel he'd climbed down before losing his leg. A loose brick had dumped him once. He poked at the bricks until he found it and stashed the bundle behind it, pushing the brick back in place. It stuck out a little, but other ones did as well. He once had the mad notion of looking behind all the others, but none were loose.

The dining hall didn't appeal to him. Ghoulish speculation about the demise of Horselli and the golem wouldn't help his mood. He meandered into the green, past where Mitryi had dragged him. *Wonder if he fixed the spring.* The weather had been growing cooler, but here in the shelter of the trees it was comfortable.

"Hello, Frederick." Katerin leaned against a tree. "We haven't talked in a while. How's your face?"

"Aches, but I've had worse."

"Good." She said, but seemed tense, uncertain. Frederick had never seen her other than composed and in control unless he counted the time on the wheel at the circus.

"What happened? The teacher looked upset." She pointed with her chin toward where the academy loomed beyond the trees.

"Lectura's golem staggered around like a drunk, then fell to pieces. He tried to put it back together but could barely make the stones shiver."

"Sounds like it was aether drunk."

"With Vassily around, it should be drunk all the time." Frederick found his own tree and sat with his back to it.

"It can't pull aether from a person or even another golem. There must have been free aether close by." She frowned. "I didn't feel anything from here, but I would only if it was large enough. Be careful, too much aether is as bad as not enough."

"I will, but I don't know what I can do. I have no idea what I would do with aether, or what it would do with me."

"Getting aether drunk would be the least of it." Katerin scowled. "Too many strange things are going on. I don't like it."

"Speaking of strange things, one of the boys in my class fell over dead. One minute he was sneering at me, the next his corpse lay on the floor devoid of aether."

"How do you know that?"

"I was there." Frederick opened his mouth to confess his part, but Katerin spoke before he could.

"I mean that the boy had no aether in him."

"Oh, the Warden came by and checked. Told us Horselli had overextended himself."

Katerin paled, then walked over to peer into Frederick's eyes, then heaved a sigh of relief. "You're all right."

"Why wouldn't I be?" Frederick's churn of emotion took on a heavier shade of fear.

"You can't die from overextending yourself, at least not like that. You'd lose consciousness before you lost the last of your aether. The Warden was covering up the true cause."

"And what would that be?" Frederick grimaces and shuffled positions, trying to get more comfortable.

"A soul stealer." Katerin's forehead wrinkled in worry. "That explains your healing not working like it should."

"What do you mean?" He looked up at her, then rubbed his neck. Katerin sighed and dropped to sit on the ground with every bit as much grace as Lylphy would have shown.

"Your eye should be normal by now, not going through shades of purple. I'd try healing you again, but it would only attract the soul stealer."

"Come on, soul stealer? It sounds like something from a play at the circus." He tried to laugh.

"There's a dangerous amount of truth in those plays." She shook her head. "You'll be fine as long as you aren't carrying a healing or the like. Make no mistake, soul stealers are real and very hard to kill. Working with aether is about pushing it into things to make them follow your will. It is your aether which controls a golem and is why golems won't listen to anyone but their creator." She spoke quickly, as if this was all information he should have had. "To kill a soul stealer, you must pull aether in. The reason using aether on a human is forbidden is it is too easy to slide from pushing to pulling since the victim's aether will resist the invasion of another's."

"Vassily did a lot of using aether on me." Frederick raised a brow. "Could he be the soul stealer?"

"He's a fool, but not a soul stealer. What he did was interfere with the working of your heart, then restore it. He used brute force, you're lucky you don't have permanent damage."

"You mean I'm lucky I have someone watching over me."

Katerin turned pink then waved her hand in dismissal.

"Be careful. I will try to find the thing and destroy it." She stood and reached hand to help Frederick. "You have some aether burn. It must have been almost on top of you."

"There was no one in the room but me and Horselli."

"That's another reason they are hard to kill." Katerin held his hand as if she'd forgotten she had it. "They may start as humans, we don't know, but by the time they are dangerous, they are floating balls of hunger."

The itch on Frederick's stomach had vanished. *So that's aether burn. Good to know.*

"I'll be careful." He squeezed her hand and let go. "I'm going to the circus today. I didn't feel up to it yesterday with my headache."

"The circus!" Katerin's eyes narrowed. "That's what I felt at the fortune teller clockwork, a nascent soul stealer. It could attach itself to the machine and eat the tiny bits of aether on the cards. When it got larger enough it left. The circus probably brought it with them." She left abruptly, leaving Frederick shaking under the trees.

He left the crystal in its hiding place and stopped at his shop just long enough to pick up his work bag. Lylphy hugged him when he showed up, leaning her head against him.

"Missed you."

"I got in a fight and didn't feel up to coming." Frederick wrapped his arms around her. "But I'm fine now."

"I'll go get Svad." She sprinted away.

Kander walked out from a different corner of the square.

"Be careful, Brass." He frowned slightly. "She's at the age where crushes are a serious thing."

"She's like a sister I never had." Frederick said, "I wouldn't dream of hurting her. But I'm not practiced in these things. I grew up alone with a lawyer for company. If you think I'm doing something wrong, let me know. Before it comes to this." He pointed at his eye.

Kander nodded and walked away. Lylphy returned with Svad in tow.

"I only have so much time to rest betw—l" Svad grinned and ran to Frederick. "Can't waste time,

Brass." He flipped onto the raised floor. Frederick followed much less smoothly.

This time, Svad allowed Frederick to successfully execute the wrestling moves, if he did them perfectly. The slightest mistake ended with him staring up at the palcan.

"Whenever we do this, I spend most of my time shorter than you." Frederick groaned and rolled to a sitting position.

"If it was anyone else," Svad grinned at him. "You might spend less time looking up to me."

"You just like having someone willing to let you throw them around." Lylphy pointed at Svad.

"Fortunately for you." Svad poked Frederick, "I have to go back to tossing around people who pay for the privilege."

"About time." Gears sauntered out. "I need Brass to work on some gears for me."

Frederick stood up and bent to pick up his bag, but Lylphy hoisted it. "I'll carry it for you."

"You have practice soon." Gears waved his hand toward the one path between tents Frederick hadn't been down yet. Lylphy pouted.

"Just for our first job then." Frederick stretched until his joints popped and the aches in his muscles eased.

She was red in the face and puffing by the time they got to the back of a game of chance booth.

"How do you carry this?"

"Practice." Frederick took it from her. "And I have no choice."

"Bye." Lylphy bolted away.

"She's going to be late." Gears shrugged and pulled open the back of the tent. "It will be a learning experience for her. There aren't many children her age in the circus. I think she's spent time following every man younger than Skattigrim."

"Is that safe?" Frederick recalled parents picking up their children at the builder's school.

"She's Skattigrim's daughter. Even if someone considered causing her harm, they would steer clear because of him. He's the only person who consistently beats Svad on the mat."

"I would die rather than hurt her. I don't have many friends."

"Right then, to work."

***

Frederick couldn't help but run through the events of the day in his head as he helped Gears fix and tune clockworks, from the games to the clattering ones at the entry.

"The clockworks are strange." Frederick sipped on a lemonade.

"Different builders have worked the circus through the years. You'd think we're all builders, but most are callers, roughnecks or performers. They have their own skills. Owner's been looking for a builder, since I'm not good with the small things. I'd have thought he would have had Baelophile corner you and make you an offer."

"Owner didn't say anything about me joining the circus." Frederick stared into his cup, not sure how he felt about it. If he could, he'd run away in an instant. The only person outside the circus he had the slightest care for was Katerin, but he was certain she'd be relieved to not have to keep putting him back together.

"You talked to Owner?" Gears went pale. "I can't recall the last person who talked to Owner himself. It's always Baelophile, I figure Owner's grooming him."

"He is a little different." Frederick finished his lemonade and put the cup in his bag.

"Different?" Gears leaned forward. "A roughneck got into it with a girl from the city we were in, maybe three years back. Anyway, the city guard come looking but the guy's nowhere to be found. It's easy to get invisible in the circus if you know how." He finished the sandwich he had in his hand. "When we were packing up, he bragged about he'd got away with it, and maybe he'd start a collection, notches on his belt so to speak." Gears rolled his eyes. "Owner had us tie him to a post, naked with a signed confession pinned to his, you know. That's one person you don't want to cross. Baelophile said Owner didn't want to leave the city with bad feelings. Nothing about the poor girl, just business." He stood up. "One more and we're done."

They wound their way through the maze of hidden paths to a tent near the entrance.

"I'm not particular about these, but it takes all kinds." He waved Frederick into the tent. "I'll be back in a bit."

The clockworks were built to titillate, and their forms left little to the imagination. Frederick set himself to ignore the look and purpose of them and focused on the workings. They were two spring clockworks and it didn't take him long to get them working right. At least he thought it was right. He had no experience to judge by.

Gears hadn't returned, and Frederick didn't want to wander off and force the man to search for him. He poked through the trunks. Some held clothes or scenery, a few had props. One trunk, the latch was stiff as if it hadn't been opened in years. He oiled it and eased the lid up and almost dropped it. The clockwork inside looked half man, half spider. The face was blank where most clockworks had at least a rudimentary attempt at features. It also looked to be even older than Taffi, but where the doll represented Lylphy's lineage, this this looked malevolent as if it had been locked in the trunk as punishment.

He almost closed it back in, but he glimpsed a crystal between the plates of the abdomen. When he took off the back, Frederick could follow how the wires from the crystal and mainspring were attached to the outside 'skin' of the creature. Any aether directed at it would be sucked in and stored in the crystal.

When he'd first lost his leg, he thought about creating a clockwork impervious to aether to wreak revenge on Vassily. He'd given it up as impossible, but here was exactly what he needed. Guiltily he took tools from his kit and disassembled the clockwork, taking each piece with a wire fixed to it. One wire looked different, but he didn't want to examine it now, when Gears could return at any minute.

Once he'd finished, Frederick closed the trunk, jamming the latch so it wouldn't open to a casual explorer. Even without its heart the thing unnerved him.

The crystal, plates, and wires he wrapped very carefully and buried them at the bottom of his pack. Then he went to wait for Gears outside the tent.

Chapter 12 Searching for the Unseeable

Katerin lay awake in the dorm room. A soul stealer—she'd told Frederick they existed, but she'd only heard old stories from the time before the retreat. If she was to hunt the thing, she needed more information, and it was only available in her mother's, *her* court. This whole thing of being queen in waiting had her freaked out.

I'm not ready. Quiet, mother said she'd take the chair until I was ready.

Finished her internal argument, Katerin got up and went to her window. It was three stories up, but that wasn't an issue, wandering teachers or students would be a problem. All clear, she climbed out set the window so she could open it from the outside, then climbed down the wall. After a quick check to be sure everything was in the right place, Katerin loped away toward the nearest entrance to the world beneath.

"Are you sure? A soul stealer?" Her mother paced on the dais while Katerin sat stiffly in the chair.

"What else could it be?" Katerin shivered. "It isn't like I'm eager to face such a creature, if there is another cause–"

"No, you're right." Her mother sighed. "It might explain part of the augury, the relentless hunger which hung over it."

"So how do I find it and destroy it?"

"You don't, you send others to track it. If you'll pardon an old woman's fears, you are too valuable to risk. There isn't a story in which half the hunting party doesn't die."

Katerin hung her head and considered her mother's advice. She hated it, wanted to brush it aside.

"You're right. But I will need to know how to defeat it in the event it finds me."

"Wise." Her mother smiled. "It is hard to set aside our own feelings when ruling. The hardest thing is to value your own life over others." She put her hand on Katerin's shoulder "The record keepers are going through the old tales and histories. When we know more, we will contact you the usual way. While you wait, refrain from any but the most essential soulwork."

"I will." Katerin pushed herself up, choking back a sob. Grief overwhelmed her, and anger. Hunger stalked her, the last of her people.

"Katerin, dear." Her mother held her like she was still the child from decades ago. "Don't try to hang on to it. Let the meaning settle in."

"I don't need to seek for the meaning." Katerin brushed tears from her eyes. "Our people are at risk. How is not clear, but I want the warning to go out. No more contact with the outside world until this evil is dead. The exploration group has been planning for years. It is time for them to put plan into action." Katerin sat up and put her fingers to her head. "Zirafia should travel with them. Instruct her in what she needs to know."

Her mother paled, but nodded and went to follow Katerin's orders.

"And me, I will return to watch." Katerin spoke to the empty room. "And pray I'm wrong."

***

No more strange deaths were reported, the golem class spent its futile hours without incident. Katerin should have been relieved, but instead tension built up in her until it took great effort to not scream at Mischa and Alikina for their shallow view of the world. Frederick spent his time split between his workshop and the circus.

The dark shop might as well have been lit by the noon sun for Katerin. Living centuries underground taught them to bypass the need for light.

On the desk lay the framework of a leg, strange, but the springs were flat or coiled and there were no gears or cogs. If it hadn't been in Frederick's shop, she wouldn't have believed he'd made it. She hoped it worked. He'd been through enough; a bit of victory would be good for him.

"You should leave with the circus. The rulers of this city have no reach past the forest." Katerin left her advice in the pitch-dark shop and returned to her increasingly uncomfortable bed.

***

Frederick took the crystals he took from the circus from the hiding spot not far from his shop, then dropped them on the table beside the leg he'd built. It worked well enough as it was. He'd look part skeleton while wearing it. Wearing it without the crystals would be the smartest thing.

Then it would only last until Vassily laid eyes on it. Like his crutches it would be twisted and useless by the end of the day. Even if Vassily had to stomp on it. The damage would show the wires and crystal and Frederick didn't want the aetheric knowing about the crystal.

He'd need to test it away from school and away from witnesses. Considering Katerin watched him constantly, that would be a problem. The place to put the crystal was in the tiny bit of plate below the knee, there to protect the joint from dust and grit.

After donning his gloves, Frederick mounted the crystal from the blatherer in its place. Wires ran from the crystal to touch every part of the leg. He'd spent hours running them to be protected and unobtrusive.

The crystal from the spiderlike clockwork he put back in the hiding place. The last one he mounted to see through, he tucked, still in its mount to be worn over his left eye, in a slot in the leg he'd created for it.

That was the easy part done.

Frederick ran a hand over his work before he went home to sleep. Tomorrow would be interesting, and unless luck ran his way, it would be his last.

***

Frederick forced himself to act no different through the day, except allowing more eagerness to flow into his face and the bounce of his foot on the floor in the third class. He grimaced and paced as the class emptied.

"Going somewhere important?" The teacher had come back out to stare suspiciously at Frederick.

"I have an appointment at the circus." Frederick said. "That's heaven compared to this place."

"Maybe, maybe." He waved Frederick off.

Frederick hopped out of the school and headed toward his rooms, turning away at the last intersection to aim for his shop. Vassily lurked back, trying to look interested in the brown flowers hanging in front of a second-hand shop.

Come on little mouse. The streets leading to the shop grew emptier. Frederick didn't know why the neighbourhood was always empty of inhabitants. Once he turned down the last alley, he sped as fast as he could without falling to his shop. Even with his rush, Frederick barely had time to put his leg on before Mitryi strolled out of the alley into the tiny square.

"Nice place," Mitryi made a show of looking around. "Vassily told me you were up to something."

Frederick stepped forward, he had to be careful not to let the motion of the spring leg unbalance him.

"Oh my, the builder has a new leg." Mitryi sneered at the creation. "But can I allow you to be unfaithful to the one which wanders?" He pointed at Frederick.

Buzzing ran through Frederick, on the cusp of pleasure or pain. As Mitryi stopped smiling, Frederick walked toward him.

"Unlike the rest of the students at that academy, I wasn't bred for stupidity." He waved at Mitryi. "You sneer at builders and yet what have you done? Have you ever made anything which you didn't dismiss at the end of class like a good little boy?"

Mitryi waved Frederick again, the buzzing grew stronger. Anger fought panic on the aetheric's face.

"I do believe the law for aetherics is the same as for golems. It is forbidden to make them intelligent. Who pulls your strings, Mitryi? Do they say you can play at being Warden someday if you behave?"

This time Mitryi pointed at the pile of rubble behind Frederick. Bead of sweats broke out on his forehead as he raised a golem from the stones.

Frederick put on his aether glass and peered at the thing looming over him. Its step made the ground shake, then it raised its hand, but the arm trembled as if the golem wanted to do something else.

"Why do golems want aether?" Frederick walked to where he could see both golem and Mitryi. The lines joining them brightened. Frederick had thought his hand glowed with aether, but Mitryi might have been a piece of the sun fallen to earth. Strangely he had no problem looking straight into the brightness. "I think they crave it so they can surpass their creators."

Frederick only intended to push Mitryi even harder, but the other boy paled, and his hand shook.

"You can't know, they were erased."

"Like poor Mischa's gran, made mad?" Fire burned in Frederick, this had started as a test of his leg and the crystal's power, but the buzz pushed him near to ecstasy and seeing fear on Mitryi's face made him laugh in delight.

The golem stomped toward Frederick, arms stretched out catch and crush him. Frederick pulled himself together and dashed through the space between the golem and Mitryi, counting on the thing being slow. The bolt of aether that hit him sent him against the wall, laughing uncontrollably. The golem disintegrated into rocks which rolled across the square.

Mitryi turned to leave, and Frederick reached out as if to stop him. He didn't expect another jolt of exquisite pleasure to run through him as Mitryi screamed and fell to the cobbles. The boy didn't glow anymore, but a glance at his own hand showed Frederick that he shone like a star.

He picked his way through the stones until he stood over Mitryi. What had he ever feared in this trembling wreck? Without the aether, he was less than nothing.

"Can't leave this mess." Frederick reformed the golem. "Take this." He handed up Mitryi's corpse. "Bury it and yourself in the river. Then you will be free to die."

Aether left him and the emptiness in him made him fall to the cobbles and weep. Only the receding shake of the ground told him the first golem he'd ever made was obeying his command.

With a huge effort, Frederick dragged himself erect. His body's strength was if anything still greater than normal, it was his soul which screamed to be filled again. He started walking after the golem, but the image of Katerin came to him.

She couldn't see him like this, and part of him could feel her coming. He jumped up and gripped the roof of his shop, then crawled up to where an empty window gaped. As Katerin turned to come down the alley. Moving at inhuman speed he rolled through the hole and fell to the floor. Clouds of dust blew up around him, and he held his breath to keep from coughing.

"Frederick!" Katerin shouted, almost screamed. "Frederick, are you here?"

She couldn't feel him then, not like he could see her with the aether glass, even through the stone of the wall. Her light made Mitryi's look like a guttering candle. The aether moved through his shop, then he heard a sigh of relief.

"Must be at the circus." Katerin talked to herself as she stood in his shop. "His leg is gone, probably he's showing off to his new friends." Her presence faded into the distance.

Frederick gasped on the floor until the hunger in him withdrew. He'd been so close to dropping on her and drinking her dry. Frederick hadn't planned on killing Vassily, just shaking him up before running away with the circus It had been bad luck for Mitryi he'd taken the bait from Vassily. Mitryi wouldn't be missed by any except those who were as bad as him. but Katerin had never been anything but a friend.

He would never attack her, never suck the last of the light out of her.

He hoped.

Chapter 13 The Foundations Shake

Katerin stopped and gasped for air. After all this time, she should have been used to the limitations of bodies in the outer world. She didn't think she'd die if this body did, but it would undo a great many careful plans.

That was the second time the soul stealer showed up near Frederick. Her mother's augury about watching began to make more sense. She needed to keep him safe from the creature or the augury she'd seen…

Katerin pushed her thoughts away from that lest thinking called it back.

The tear in the world's soul echoed as far as the park where she walked with Mischa and Akilina, what were they going to think of her sprint away from them? She might have to ease their memories, though she hated to do it. It could have severe consequences for both involved.

She'd never imagined anything like the soul eater. What else could it be? Now she understood her mother's insistence that she not hunt it alone. The stories where half the hunters survived may have been optimistic.

"Katerin!" The girls ran up to her. "Whatever happened? You looked terrified!" Mischa gasped as she clasped Katerin to her.

"Did you see a shade?" Akilina trembled. "My gran was terrified of shades. She said they came up from the underworld to steal souls."

"It must have been something like that." Katerin shuddered. "It was like something horrible ran claws through my heart."

"Don't encourage her." Mischa wagged her finger to scold Katerin, but her face showed a mix of fear and delight. "You can't talk like that, or they'll send you away like they did Akilina's gran."

"They?" Katerin let go of Mischa and stepped back.

"The hidden kings," Mischa dropped her voice to a whisper, though no one moved near them on the street. "They run everything from the shadows. Displease them and you vanish. Not a word, and it's as if you never existed."

"They sound like Akilina's shades." Katerin smiled. "Don't we aetheric run Lexburgh?"

"Be honest." Mischa frowned. "You might be ok, but Akilina and I can barely dress ourselves. The boys aren't any different. How would we run anything?"

"That's silly," Akilina said. "We girls won't run anything. We'll marry some handsome boy and go to parties. I wouldn't want to run anything. It would be too much like work."

The girls argued in hushed whispers all the way back to the dorm, completely confusing themselves, Katerin's running away forgotten.

Katerin wanted nothing more than to visit her mother and feel her arms, but going to the world below used aether, and she couldn't take the slightest risk that the monster could find the entrance. Echoes of the augury ran through her, and she shuddered.

*****

Frederick put the leg in the room where he'd hid. From the lack of disturbance in the dust, it was as good a place as any. Even without it he could climb to the roof. He'd done so to patch a couple of leaks. It would get rainier soon and fixing the roof in the rain didn't sound like fun.

The awful hunger in him had curled around his heart, but it slept for now. He limped home with his crutch, feeling the loss of his leg all over again.

His dreams were haunted by a huge spider which scuttled through the circus devouring his friends, Lylphy screamed for him as she melted away, more like wax than a person.

Hunger woke him, but though he ate a most of a loaf and large plate of cheese and cold sausage, it didn't go away. It didn't want food. Frederick picked up a crutch from the collection he had at the door, a reminder of Vassily.

Frederick had felt guilty over Horselli's death. It had been an accident and Frederick bore him no malice. The boy only followed the rule of his class. Mitryi's death was more complicated. He'd been lured to his death. Yes, he would have killed Frederick in an instant without regret. But was he really the enemy?

The line between them had blurred. Frederick understood Mitryi better than he imagined he could.

The academy was in chaos with groups of boys huddled whispering rumours. Mitryi had eloped with a girl from the circus. He'd been found with a stake through his heart. Not one murmur suggested he slept under the mud of the river, covered by a huge mound of rock. Vassily hadn't showed up.

Eventually they were shepherded into class, Professeur fussing about them as if it was the first day of term again. He began a lecture which had no connection with the one from yesterday. His drone was even duller and more lifeless, as if without Vassily there was no point.

Frederick guessed without the need to maintain the fiction of aetheric superiority, the entire first year would have been dismissed and left to fend for themselves.

Where Professeur had sunk into apathy, Lectura tortured the class with the brutal resolution to make them replace the missing Vassily. His golem gave up any pretense of picking who to punish and ran amok through the class cracking shins and shrieking as if it was being tortured. It tackled Frederick carrying him to the ground with its surprising weight. It jumped on his neck, cackling, then walked up his body to wrap it hands around his throat. Lectura's grimace could not be described as any human expression.

The golem might have killed him there, if Katerin hadn't walked out of the forest. She stalked up to Lectura and slapped him, when he would have retaliated, she said something too soft for Frederick to hear over the grinding of the golem's joints. Lectura wilted, the golem crawled off Frederick and the two of them walked away. The class cleared out, complaining loudly about bruises and scrapes.

"You are always saving me." Frederick stared at her from the ground. "I hope you don't regret it."

"Why would I regret what is the right thing?" Katerin frowned down at him.

Frederick wanted to confess, to explain the whole thing, let her put it right, as she always had. The hunger choked him, silencing his voice.

"Young lady." The Warden walked around the corner to confront them. "Why have you disturbed the teaching of my students?"

"Teaching?" Katerin pointed to Frederick. "The golem was on his chest hands on his throat. I doubt there is a boy in the class without bruises."

"It is my school, discipline of students and teachers is my concern, not a truant from her own school."

"How much did you get for the selling of your soul?" Katerin met the Warden's eyes. "Are you still content with your bargain?"

"I will speak with your headmistress. Such insolence will not go unpunished." The Warden's face had turned red, his hands shook.

"You do that, I will send the lines she will make me write." Katerin walked back into the forest without so much as looking at Frederick.

"I will lash you until you are bloody, damn them and their schemes." The Warden moved as if to kick him; but glanced at the forest.

The shaking wasn't rage but fear? Why would he be afraid of her? The only reason Frederick could come up with was she stood closer to the mysterious *them* who ran the school and watched.

"Never know who's watching, do you?" Frederick forced his body to sit up. In a year or two he'd try getting up on his foot. "I don't know what your bosses have in mind for me, what deals they've made with my father, but I quit. If they want me in this hellhole, they'll need to carry me in and prop up my corpse."

"If you stop attending, your guardian will face severe punishment." The Warden almost sounded like he was begging.

"He made his deal with the devil, just as you did." Frederick used his crutch to lever himself up. He only had one leg and it didn't want to hold him. *Get me to my shop, then you'll have company.*

One hop at a time, Frederick turned his back on the academy.

He stopped in at Granfle's office. The clerks stared at him wide-eyed, probably wondering how to escape.

"I have a message for Granfle." Frederick ground out the words. The hunger lurked behind his eyes, sending shooting pains through his head.

"You can tell me yourself." Granfle came through a door, closing it behind him. As always, he looked immaculate and in control.

"I quit." Frederick turned and began the painful process of getting out of the office.

Granfle grabbed his shoulder.

"What do mean quit? You can't, the agreement—"

"I quit. I didn't sign the agreement, you did. You fulfill it. I'm done."

"I am still your guardian." Granfle tightened his grip on Frederick's shoulder. "You will attend if I have tie you and hire men to carry you."

"No." Frederick let slip his reins on the hunger. Without the crystal the drain wasn't fast enough to kill Granfle before he staggered back, grey-faced and clutching his heart.

Frederick left the office, his leg a bit stronger. Since he was moving better, he collected the few things he needed from his rooms. His workshop he had already stripped bare, just as well; he didn't think he could carry any metal or tools.

As he dragged himself down the alley, the brief burst of wellness having fled, sounds of metal clinking made him stop. Frederick eased himself to the opening into the square. A man in ragged clothes had dumped all the brass and copper parts on the ground and picked through them mumbling.

"That's mine." Frederick pushed himself into the square. The thieving man looked up, then charged, a brass plate held like a knife in his hand. Frederick crouched as Svad had taught him. He caught the thief's arm, twisted and threw, putting all his anger and pain into it.

The man hit the corner where the alley joined the square, a crack echoed in the courtyard. Frederick hopped over and lowered himself. The man gasped, his face stretched in agony, but he still looked at Frederick with hope.

"This will help with the pain." Frederick put his hand on the man's heart and unleashed the hunger.

***

Frederick made his way to the circus, stuffing the guilt down deep in his gut, burying it, like he had hidden the vagrant a couple of blocks from his workshop. He'd wound through back alleys, but as usual nobody moved there or on the street. *Why would a whole neighbourhood be abandoned?*

Kander met him at the gate.

"Owner wants to see you."

Frederick took a breath. *Just coincidence.* He followed the young man. Kander wasn't as tall as Skattagrim, but the easy confidence in his walk made Frederick think he wouldn't want to tangle with him, yet he didn't look any older than Mityri.

Kander held up the side of the tent for Frederick, then walked away.

"Come in, come in." The warped voice of his father pulled him into the darkness. "You've been a naughty boy, thinking of running away with the circus."

"Like father like son." Frederick restrained a sigh when his father didn't mention aether. Why would he?

"More than you realize." The whisper came from behind him. The slightest scrabble reached his ears. "You are no longer welcome here. You have a job to do, and playing at builder in the circus is not it."

The words hit Frederick like a punch. He lunged forward to grab his father and shake sense into him. His hand brushed against metal before a blow sent him tumbling back.

"Foolish child." His father hissed.

"Why?" Frederick climbed to his feet deliberately ignoring the pain in his ribs.

"You are the key." The words came from far away as if his father feared another attack. "Your mother was a builder. I...am not."

"What are you then?" Frederick threw his words into the darkness.

"That doesn't matter."

Frederick's body turned and walked out of the tent. He fought whatever commanded him, but uselessly, he couldn't even shout in frustration.

Outside the fence, control returned to him. He pounded on the door, yelling for it to open. Nothing, not even someone to tell him to go away. *Lylphy*, he needed to say goodbye.

Frederick joined the line at the main gate, maybe the word hadn't spread yet. He held out his coin to pay for entry. The man in blue waved it away.

"Sorry, orders from Baelophile, you aren't allowed in. Owner said he don't want a fight with the aetheric here. Please..." The man shook.

When did I become that scary?

"Won't cause you any trouble." Frederick clapped him on the shoulder. "Not your fault." He walked away, his leg sending him the barest tingle from the people in line.

He wandered the city until he thought his leg would give out. Ironic that his metal leg was now more reliable than his flesh and bone. The golem had damaged something.

There weren't many people on the streets. With all its wide streets, Lexburgh felt empty. Frederick wished he could have seen it in its heyday with clockwork carriages and fountains. Before the aetheric had betrayed them and taken over the city, pushing the builders to the slums.

But the downfall of the builders couldn't have emptied so much of Lexburgh. Something else was happening. Maybe the plot he was forced to be part of explained it. Right now, he didn't care.

Frederick found a new place to live by finding a building with boarded up windows. Dust lay thick on the floor. A board helped him shovel most of it out into another room. His had a table and chair. All he needed. He put his work bag on the table and pulled out pieces. There were no more long bars or heavy flat springs among his stock. He'd had them made with the last of his coin from his commissions. Maybe he didn't need them.

He worked on a brace for his weak leg until he couldn't see, then slept under the table. In the morning he picked up where he'd left off. By the afternoon he had a contraption of brass plates with tight spring on either side of his knee. He'd picked them up from the circus, parts they didn't need. When he'd finished, he fixed it on his right leg and tried walking. It balanced the left much better.

"Maybe the golem only finished the job." Frederick muttered. The circus should have been feeding him now. He should be laughing with Lylphy or working with Gears on keeping the clockwork circus going. His fist clenched, his father still determined to use Frederick's life for whatever twisted goal he and the true rulers of Lexburgh had cooked up.

It had to be a long-term goal. The course of Frederick's life had been set when his father ran away, leaving him with Granfle. He hadn't listened much, but the lawyer had admonished him by saying he was going to the most prestigious school in Lexburgh.

He wasn't going to unravel a plot a decade in the making by sitting feeling sorry for himself. They should have let him join the circus. Now boredom and hunger were going to be his constant companions. Destroying the people who'd made his life hell should keep boredom at bay.

As for the hunger, Frederick's stomach growled in concert with the monster in his heart. He knew how to deal with one of them, but he'd need the parts hidden away near his old shop. Hiding the tool bag and other pieces took a little time and ingenuity so the dust didn't give them away. But he was a builder, he made it work.

Outside he strolled along the street. A few people gave him odd looks, one stopped him to ask if he was from the circus. Red rage blossomed in Frederick and only the watching people kept him from ripping the aether from the woman and leaving her on the street.

The bundle was where he'd left it. Frederick put inside his shirt. To think he'd been nervous around this. It was going to save his life.

He would need brass and copper, some spring steel.

***

Dan Stilli who usually supplied Frederick with materials welcomed him.

"Wow." Dan circled him. "That's some work. There's people who pay to wear such things."

"They'd cut off their leg to walk on a skeleton?" Frederick frowned.

"Well, maybe not that, but the brace on your knee, and there are others who have lost limbs."

"Let's make a trade." Frederick calculated quickly. "You find the customers and supply the metal and you keep six tenths of the price. I'll take three of my tenths in metal and one in coin."

"Are you sure?" Dan tilted his head.

"You are supplying the metal and doing the leg work. All I need to do is do what I do."

"Done." Dan put out his hand. Frederick took the barest tingle from him. He needed him alive.

"It would be easiest to do the fittings here." Frederick peered into the depths of the shop. "There's no shortage of space."

"True enough, business isn't as busy my father talked about it. To be honest, this deal of ours is what I needed to stay afloat."

"I'm glad." Frederick straightened. "If I'm going to be doing this on commission, I will need some materials to experiment with. You can take the cost out of my first three tenths."

"Let me show you what I have in stock." Dan led him back into the gloom.

Chapter 14 The Hunger

Frederick woke shaking uncontrollably, a beast in his gut crying to ravage the city. The idea of killing someone whose only crime was being near him made him sick, but the hunger would consume him if he didn't feed it soon.

He climbed to his feet and brushed off the dust. The work he'd started with the metal from Dan lay arranged on the table. The large crystal from the old clockwork in the trunk lay in the center, wires ran from it to bands to put on his arms, to his legs, up his back to the aether glass. Frederick had been working from instinct, with no clear idea of what it did.

The idea of putting it on made him shudder, but why build it to not use it? He sighed and peeled off his clothes, then strapped the brass breast plate on. The harness for it held a back plate of copper. The wires ran from the shoulders of the harness along his arms to a band which fit above his elbow to another around his wrist. Others from the bottom to connect to his legs. The one up to his head he'd anchored in a hat he'd found, round with enough space for him to put a steel cap inside. When he put the aether glass on, it would connect with the hat.

He dressed carefully so to not disturb the contraption, but it faded out of his mind as soon as he slipped out of his room to make his way to the street. The tingling in his limbs began immediately. There weren't many people on the street, but many who did walk past him put hands to their head as if struck by a sudden pain.

The hunger wanted to devour them all, but Frederick restrained it, let it feed on the trickle of aether from the citizens of the city. It sulked but pulled back.

Why would such things be in the circus? None of the circus people were aetheric. Builders, workers, performers of all kind, but none who needed aether. They were old, maybe from a time when aetheric used them to harvest slivers of soul from everyone who visited. The thought didn't bother him, and that worried him. How much had he already changed? Katerin described soul stealers as horrific monsters.

I'm not a monster. I won't become one.

Even with the hunger chained and bound, Frederick didn't dare stay in any one place too long, or those around him grew pale and complained of illness. He'd never spent much time exploring more than his little corner of Lexburgh. Broad streets led him to a district of fine stores. Clothes like what Vassily wore, thoughtlessly rich, wasteful of fabric with capes and folds. The women's dresses were layers upon layers, until Frederick didn't know how anyone would wear them, yet he saw some on the street.

This quarter was more populated with aetheric bustling importantly while craftspeople served them obsequiously, overjoyed at the chance to close to the ruling class. A few advertised an eye for fashion, or an ability to bake flawless bread and treats.

What makes the builders and aetheric special? It is almost like we are different kinds, builders to make life easier and aetheric to claim ease for themselves. The aetheric ability ran in families. All the students were related in some way. A claim to a connection to the Lord Mayor's line was something to brag about, no matter how far back.

Frederick had never met enough builders to know if it was the same. Did they only wed other builders? He'd never even thought of it until now. Even though a part of him flushed with a rosy glow when he considered Katerin, he had no idea of what any closer relationship would look like.

His father had said his mother was a builder, what was his father? An aetheric? It might explain his presence at the academy, but the invisible rulers had plans for him too. What could they need from a builder?

His father had claimed he was the key, and something about phemerals being the real power. He'd never heard the word before.

His hunger gobbled the more abundant aether and the tingle became a stream of pleasure, tinged with pin and needles of pain. The aetheric didn't pale or slow in their pace, so Frederick didn't restrain the beast. His face grew warm from the flow, and he had to concentrate to not stagger drunkenly.

Enough. Frederick closed the gates, and the sensations dropped to a manageable level. *How am I doing this?* The image of the endless days focusing on a pile of rocks to make it come alive came to him. That discipline is what served him now. *Was that deliberate?* Frederick hovered between terror and rage at the idea that his torture at the academy was coldly planned for the day he'd become a soul stealer. Who knew how soul stealers were made?

I'm not a soul stealer. Not yet, and I won't be.

"You!" A rough hand landed on his shoulder and spun him around. Lectura stood in front of him, red and stinking of drink. The golem beside him gripped Frederick's leg. Was it growing larger?

Lectura's fist striking his face distracted Frederick. He shook his head. The aetheric walking past moved to create a space in their flow, but none stopped to watch or remonstrate one of their own.

"Do you really plan to make a scene on the street?" Frederick raised an eyebrow. He'd felt the blow, but no pain and no damage. Lectura stepped back, confusion written on his face in wrinkled brow. He put hands to his head, then as if a switch had been activated, he turned away.

"Come then, and we'll make our scene in private." The voice didn't sound like Lectura though it came from his mouth, but Frederick shook off the golem, now standing up to his waist, and followed.

Lectura walked straight, far different from the golem like shuffle he usually had. Maybe that was an act for the students. Yet Frederick had never seen anything in Lectura to suggest he was capable of such an act.

As they stepped into a tiny park surrounded by a high hedge, the golem threw itself at Frederick, claws tearing through Frederick's clothes.

He unleashed the hunger and put his aether glass on. Lectura barely shone brighter than any non-aetheric, but his golem burned with red light. Lines of power ran from both into the distance. Lectura threw another punch. Frederick ignored it and gripped the man's neck. The bracer on his wrist heated sending waves of power up his arm, making him shudder. There was far more aether than the man should have had.

A blow from the golem sent Frederick reeling. If he hadn't had the steel cap, his skull would have been crushed. He reached out to take control of the golem, but it fought him. Lectura lay on the grass struggling to climb to his feet. The golem stood taller than Frederick now. The flow of aether in it looked more like a human's. He didn't have time to worry about it as the thing charged.

Frederick crouched low and caught the stone creature with his shoulder at the thing's waist. He lifted it high with impossible strength and slammed it down on Lectura. The line of power to the man vanished, and an echo of pain came back along the thread of aether controlling the golem. Frederick took hold of the thread and sucked on the aether. The connection snapped, and he staggered a moment from the shock.

Several aether sources, bright as Vassily converged on him. The hunger wanted to stay and feed, but Frederick already fought to stay in control. Lectura had tossed his coat on the hedge before attacking. Frederick wrapped it around him and bolted from the park.

At least he'd intended on running, instead he jumped in a low arc to crash into the wall of a building outside the park. He hardly paused before jumping to the roof, then fleeing across the city at monstrous speed.

***

At his home Frederick collapsed on the floor gasping, every part of him but his metal leg hurt, and even that had bent out of shape. The aether flowed though him like a maelstrom, sucking him in. He closed his eyes and took control, though knives of pain stabbed through him. He had no notion of how to heal, the energy slipped out of his control whenever he turned it on himself.

Instead, Frederick worked on the brass, copper and steel he had. Gears and springs to take the flow of aether and use it channel the force of movement off his flesh and bone, armour to protect him from physical attacks, all hooked into the crystal on his chest. He took the one out of his metal leg and formed a brass glove with the crystal in the palm, copper wires running up to each fingertip.

When he had finished, he stood and moved around. Exhaustion struck him like a blow. He'd been so full of aether, and now it was all but gone. With the last he fashioned a tiny golem to watch over him.

He woke weeping, a hole in him which swallowed all hope in the future. Frederick rolled onto his back and ignored the tears running off his face.

"It's the aether." He forced the words past the lump in his throat. "It isn't real." Reflexively he reached out to steal the pitiful amount of aether in the golem. Yesterday, he'd wandered thoughtlessly through the city, barely hiding the clockworks on him. Today he needed to be more careful. There were people hunting him.

The red threads of power confused him. Aether's light was colourless, what had been done to it to change its nature? Something else worried him. Both

Lectura and the golem were controlled from somewhere else. Some place shielded from his aether glass. Whoever was at the other end of that strand knew a lot more about aether than he did.

Frederick dressed in the rags that were left of his clothes, then put Lectura's coat on. It would stick out as much here as his brass and copper, but it hid most of his clockwork. Out on the street Frederick flipped the aether glass over his eye. He saw more than just forward through the crystal. A picture of the city formed in his mind. Most of it all but devoid of power, but one section beckoned with a siren call. His feet carried him toward the aetheric quarter before he'd made the decision.

Just enough so I can think clearly. No more. The hunger deep in his soul laughed at him. As he got close to the quarter, people looked at him oddly. Frederick stopped to examine himself in a store window. Under the hat, his aether glass glinted over his left eye, copper and brass winked from beneath the coat. His metal leg and knee brace gleamed through tears in his pants.

Bright aether blinked into being not more than a hundred yards from him. Others followed farther away, but coming quickly.

Frederick took aether from those around him, people dropped to the street. He wrenched the beast back before it took their lives. He had enough for now.

Running with the changes in his legs was easy, the metal taking the force of his feet hitting the cobbles. Ahead the aether sun resolved into a man a bit younger than the Warden. He carried a sword like he knew how to use it. Frederick charged, but the man spun out of the way, the slash from the sword cut the back of the coat in half. Frederick dropped it. The hunger twisted his mouth into a smile which could just as well be the snarl of a dog.

"Untrained, undisciplined dog." The man lifted his sword and threw a line of aether at Frederick, red like the ones controlling Lectura and his golem. Frederick snatched with his gloved hand and went to his knees as his aether was pulled out through the red line. The man stepped forward his sword in position for the first cut.

The hunger in Frederick howled in rage. Frederick didn't know if he howled along with it, but he gripped the thread tighter and fought the pull to a standstill, the man's eyes opened in shock and his attack faltered. Frederick lunged in close to make his response. He didn't have a sword but got close enough to slam the crystal on his palm over the swordsman's heart.

He no longer fought for aether, only to keep from getting drunk on it. The corpse had hardly hit the cobbles before the next came from behind, sword held ready to slash at Frederick's neck. When his gloved hand gripped the fallen man's sword it cut channels in it to steal aether.

A net of red thread hung over him. Frederick ignored it, spinning under the other man's cut to lunge and pierce his heart. The sword scraped on armour and the tip snapped. Frederick's momentum carried him into a collision with the other. His opponent's sword dropped to the street with a clang, and the man clapped his hands on either side of Frederick's head. The draw of aether was agony. Frederick punched with the sword, connecting just below the man's chin. Blood and aether hemorrhaged, the blood pooled on the street, the aether pulled in by his hunger.

With the consumption of two aetheric in as many minutes, Frederick staggered, unable to control his limbs. He laughed wildly and picked up the other sword in his left hand and screamed a challenge to the heavens. The approaching aether slowed and stopped in a circle around him. The monster in him didn't care, but Frederick recognized a disciplined action.

Time to go. His hunger growled and fought, but Frederick prevailed, then leaped up and forward just as bright red beams of energy met where he'd stood seconds before. The monster retreated and Frederick fled over the tops of buildings; the hunters pursued him, not getting close enough for him to attack, but easily following him.

Frederick came to a street filled with dead clockworks, their gears long fused, corrosion streaking them like tears. He threw out a wave of aether which rolled over the clockworks, bringing them to life. They moved to attack the hunters. While almost devoid of aether, Frederick scrambled on foot into the alleyways. An opening into the sewers beckoned, and he dropped into the stench, then limped as fast as he could away from the chaos behind him.

***

Katerin looked up from the endless lines the headmistress had assigned her. A wave of aether crashed through the city. The cry of souls at the edge of death made her wince and cling to the desk until her knuckles were white. She was a healer, and to ignore the pain made tears run from her eyes.

"So, the weight of your actions has finally set in." The headmistress sat oblivious to the turmoil. "You may go, but never let me hear of a such a thing again."

Katerin almost begged her to assign more lines, anything to keep her in this room and away from the horror outside. Instead, she walked with dignity until she was out of sight, then sprinted across the city. She'd foolishly thought she was the only one to be able to use aether to move, but a confusion of sources converged on a spot in the aetheric section of the city. One aetheric died, the ripple of his passing ripping at her soul. Then another, and Katerin missed her jump to crash painfully on a roof top. She rolled until she came up hard against the wall enclosing the roof, once a raised garden, now dry and brown.

She couldn't move, bones in her weak body had shattered. As she sent aether to knit them together, she tracked the battle, a huge red cloud of aether stood in the center of a circle of clean sources. Then they sent red beams toward the cloud and Katerin decided they weren't that clean after all. The soul stealer, she was sure the red cloud was that evil being, jumped away from the converging attack and fled. It had to be free of a body, even she would not move so quickly in flesh and blood. The circle gave chase. All that was missing was the baying of hounds.

Then the red cloud exploded in a wave, fragments of it moving slowly, then with increasing speed. She had to see with her eyes. Even with bones not fully knit Katerin moved quickly toward the now multitude of red sources.

On a high roof overlooking what had once been a grand boulevard, Katerin watched, her mouth hanging open.

Clockworks gave battle to the men with swords who also glowed with power. The aetherics dispatched the clockworks with both sword and power, but they were outnumbered, and more clockwork golems clanked toward them from all directions. A golem crushed one of the men and shrieked in triumph before being shattered by a line of aether from another man. Other aetherics came at a run, attacking the golems, returning them to lifeless piles of metal. The clockwork golems didn't die quietly, at least three other aetheric died under their hands.

When the last golem fell, Katerin shuddered, holding herself in place. The aetheric had their own healers. She couldn't come to their attention, not and live. In the world beneath, aether was only used at need, soul work they called it, as it could build or destroy a soul. The chaos and violence she'd witnessed was beyond her experience. If these people caught the slightest hint of her people's existence it would be bloody slaughter.

The soul stealer had escaped, vanishing without a trace as if it had evaporated.

Katerin lay on the rooftop until long after dark finishing the repairs to her body. She'd be late for evening roll call. Breaking curfew would mean more lines. Suddenly the stullifying boredom of repeated lines looked good to Katerin. At least it was safe and didn't tear at her soul like the claws of a ravening beast.

Slowly she travelled back to the dorm, walking in late and getting scolded for being very late for curfew. Katerin basked in the ordinary sound of the matron's voice.

"Yes, matron. I will report to you in the morning to begin my lines."

The matron looked at her oddly as, in spite of her best effort, Katerin couldn't keep the relief from her voice.

Chapter 15 Battle Plans

In a barracks hidden from the rest of Lexburgh, young men dressed their wounds and mourned their fallen.

"Warden present." The youngest of them and nearest the door shouted out the words and the men came to attention. Pain of body and spirit pushed away.

"Report." The Warden's voice was soft, but no one in that room would mistake it for weak.

"Antonov was closest to the void beast. He attacked with drawthreads and sword together." The newly oldest of them spoke in clipped tones. "It was a flawless attack, he's not the lead hunter of voids for no reason." A hint of pride slipped into the oldest's voice.

"Yet he failed."

"The void was taken down by the drawthreads, but as Antonov moved to kill it, it reversed the flow on the thread, even then it should have fallen, but it dodged the sword as if it had trained for the maneuver. Antonov died between one breath and the next. We are guessing a holding crystal made to absorb as well as store."

"It has been done." The Warden nodded his head. "Difficult and dangerous both. Continue."

"Krovost ordered the circle, then closed in to delay the void beast until we were set. He knew the risk. We expected more time. He died after he missed his first slash. We found a broken sword, it had been used to cut Krovost's throat." The oldest shuddered and had to breathe in slowly. The Warden waited impassively.

"Under my order we formed the circle and fired the net. If it had hit, it would have held it and drained in seconds."

"If it had hit."

"The void beast jumped a second before the beams knit then fled at high speed. We followed as we could in the semi-circle we were taught for attack and defense as a unit."

"I am familiar with the formation." There might have been the slightest twitch of the Warden's mouth.

"Then..." the oldest struggled for words. "It was if the city took arms against us. Clockworks attacked. They were mindless, but in such numbers..." He trailed off and hung his head.

"The void beast is still out there." The Warden paced in front of the line of young men. "This is not an unthinking creature as you are used to hunting. It is planning, reacting like a human. You will patrol in pairs. Your first task is to rid the city of any clockwork which may be used against you."

"Your pardon, Warden." The youngest put his hand on his chest and knelt.

"Speak."

"Something watched us as we fought the clockworks. A powerful source of aether, but well cloaked."

"Then how were you able to detect it?"

"Sir, it was in pain, psychic pain." Vassily met his gaze. "I believe it is trained as a healer, and withholding aid made its shield waver."

"Interesting." The Warden stood still for a long moment, then looked around as if he'd just arrived. "The void beast is our first concern, but if you happen upon this watching healer, bring it in." He walked out of the room. The young men held their attentive pose for a count of sixty beats of a heart. Then the oldest relaxed and the other returned to discussion of the battle.

***

Katerin returned to her room to find a visitor.

"Your guise needs work." She went to the sideboard and heated water to make tea.

"No one saw me." Zirafia said and adjusted her features.

"You don't know if anyone saw you." Katerin poured the tea and handed the cup to her cousin.

"These people? They barely see past the end of their noses."

"These people faced a soul stealer and almost won. They worked in unison, disciplined even when one of their own fell."

Zirafia lowered her eyes. "I will be more careful, my Queen."

"Please do," Katerin said. "I would hate to lose you."

"But you are sending me away." Zirafia almost wailed.

"Next to me, you are the closest to the royal line." Katerin caught her cousin's chin and held it so she couldn't look away. "I know it is going to be a hard trip, and dangerous." She let go of Zirafia. "That's why I need you on the trek. You will take the Stone of Meirthign with you."

"That's a Queen's stone." Zirafia knelt. "I am not ready. I can't. I won't." She glared defiantly at Katerin.

"You will." Katerin's voice had no give in it. "We are entering the most dangerous time in our history since the breaking."

Zirafia's features collapsed. "As you will." She threw herself at Katerin and clutched her tightly. Katerin held her until the sobs subsided.

"These bodies are strange and weak." Katerin stroked Zirafia's hair. "But at times like this, they can be oddly comforting."

"Oh, I have a message from the Regent." Zirafia wiped her face and hiccupped. "They have learned more of the battles against soul stealers."

"To do battle with one, means you become what you fight." Katerin put her cup down. "I watched the truth with my own eyes. Those who fought the soul stealer used tainted aether."

"The stories say that while some of the hunters returned triumphant, none lived within a sun's turn. They walked into the desert or gave up their souls. The Regent begs you not to fight it. Let these others fight the battle."

"I will not run to battle." Katerin stood and looked out the window. "But something tells me the time will come when I will not have a choice."

"An augury?" Zirafia whispered.

"Yes." Katerin said. "The reason you travel to find new places to live."

"My Queen, I will do what I must, and someday we will meet again and exchange tales." Zirafia put her hand over her heart.

"Thank you, cousin. Now you must return before light. It is more dangerous than you can imagine here."

***

Zirafia climbed down the wall and ran for the entrance to the world beneath. Katerin's words terrified her, and her breath came in gasps, her heart racing. One street from the entrance she stopped and gathered herself. She couldn't return like a scared child.

When she was ready, she made her way in the shadows toward the entrance. There was a time when they hadn't needed to hide them, but centuries had passed in this world since then. She found the archway. Anyone else who walked beneath it would end up in an empty temple, glass hanging in the windows like broken teeth. It made her sad, but in the brief time she'd been here, most of this world had made her sad.

Raising her hands, she started forming the way. Then a thread of aether wrapped around her and pulled at her soul. She screamed in agony.

"Looks like we caught your watcher." A rough voice came from behind her, but she couldn't think. The torment of that red thread stole her strength. Her form wavered and the two behind gasped. For a second, she almost broke free, then the pain hammered down leaving her trembling on the street.

"What is that thing?" The voice held fear and wonder.

"It is from the forbidden stories." The other replied, and the thread tightened until Zirafia's whole world was red misery.

Then the thread snapped, and she almost lost consciousness. Lying with her cheek on the cobbles she could see a thing surrounded by a red nimbus. It threw one of the humans against the wall to strike with a sickening thud before crumpling to the ground. It held the other and drained the soul from it before tossing it aside to land on the other.

Soul stealer. Zirafia's panic increased until spots floated in front of her. She released her form and regained control over her emotions.

The soul stealer stared at her one eye brown, the other glowing red.

"Katerin?" It rasped, the human words struck her uncomfortably as if they were blades.

"No, a friend." Zirafia said. "Please take me and leave her alone. We need her."

"Is this what she looks like too?"

Zirafia winced and nodded, hating herself for the betrayal.

"You are beautiful." The human whispered. The red around it swirled like a live thing. "Go, go now and don't come back." It fell to its knees and gripped its head. Zirafia gasped and scrambled away. It held fragments of what was very similar to the Broken Stone of the Queen; but filled with hunger and hate. She jumped to her feet, opened the gate, then fled through letting it close behind her.

She ran until she reached the Queen's Hall. The Regent sat on the chair.

"My Queen," Zirafia threw herself on the floor in abjection. "The soul stealer, it *saw* me, it thought I was Katerin, then it let me go. It's outside the gate."

"Peace." The Regent walked down the steps, then knelt beside Zirafia. "What is done, is done. There is no telling how it will end. Regain yourself, you have work to do." She put a ring with a large crystal set in it on Zirafia's finger. Strength and courage flowed into her to replace what she'd lost to the thread.

"We leave immediately. Inform all who would travel. Any who are not ready within the turn will be left behind." Zirafia stood straight though her heart ached.

"Need you rush so?" The Regent frowned.

"As the stone was broken, our house is sundered." Pain like nails shot through her head, but Zirafia stood and saluted the Regent as an equal. "Close the gate, or you will grieve it."

"If we close the gate, Katerin will be alone in the outer world without a way to return."

"You will do what you do, and there will be loss either way."

"We will set a watch."

Zirafia left to organize her people.

Only when they were well on their way, their home lost in the mist did she feel the twinge where the thread had bound her and realized she should have warned the Regent about the red aether. Tears fell, but she didn't look back. Their fate had been sundered from hers.

"Set watch." She ordered her guards. "There are red threads which eat souls. If they exist in the outer world, they may here. The only defense is to render the attacker unconscious. Show neither hesitation nor mercy."

Children cried behind her; mothers comforted them. Each carried what they could, and they must live off that.

Katerin, stay safe, and one day our children will greet each other.

***

Shadows crawled across the courtyard. The arch let moonlight through from the temple. Vassily lay holding onto life with a fierce grip. He had to report.

Footsteps scraped on the road into the courtyard, and two of his companions entered.

"Vassily," one shouted and ran to him. "What do we do? Aether's blight, but you're in bad shape."

"Forget that, I must report, then I can live or die."

They poured as much aether into Vassily as they could spare, but still he leaked light like a sieve. One ran for their barracks, spending aether recklessly to get there in time.

"Hold on, Vassily." The one left behind kept, trying to stem the flood. Crashing footsteps announced the Warden's coming. The man ran into the yard, made straight for Vassily.

"Report." The Warden's voice was harsh, but his hand held the boy's head gently. Vassily knew his commander honoured him.

Vassily whispered what he'd seen, as impossible as it sounded. His commander's face never changed as Vassily's voice weakened and stumbled through his report. When he'd finished, he kept his eyes on his commander as the last of his soul bled out. The Warden never blinked or looked away, though his eyes betrayed him with tears.

***

The Warden stood and didn't give the Lord Mayor son's body a second glance.

"Post a guard. Two at all times. You are to watch and observe. Do not engage, do not even be seen."

He walked away certain they would obey him to the death. It was how they were trained. Wolves hidden in the herd.

"LeSille." The Warden allowed anger and hate to fill his voice. "They insisted you could be broken, that you would be what we needed to restore the city." His fist clenched. "There will be a price for their failure. Then I will exact my price from you."

He marched to the academy and climbed to his tower room. Two years lost to them. They would want to rush the younger ones into place. The Warden looked out the window over the green to where Katerin hid. He wouldn't rush. Plans made in haste were doomed to failure.

Failure would not be allowed. He returned to his desk and thought how a builder become void beast and a creature out of myth could be turned to his advantage. Time a stronger hand took control before they were all dead.

***

Frederick stumbled through the sewers banging into the walls, impervious to the stench. The hunger fought him, punished him. That creature who had sounded like Katerin when she called. The light from her held an entirely different quality than the aether of other's he'd seen. Like Katerin's, it outshone the sun.

The thing had cowered, black as night with eyes like the moon. He was stunned by the beauty, as if he'd come across a rare treasure. The hunger in him demanded he feast, she would have put up no resistance, but Frederick held back until it had fled through the archway.

The sewer came out to drip its viscous liquid into the black mud of the river, not far from the circus. He looked over at it. It might as well have been a different world. Aether flowed with the moving crowds even this late. He was forbidden entry by his father, another creature of the darkness, but a creature who held answers. There was no beauty in either of them.

I have a few matters to deal with here. Frederick shook his fist at the wall. Then I'm coming after you.

Chapter 16 Plague

Rumours of plague went through Lexburgh like wildfire. From the accounts Frederick heard, people were dropping all over the city. The disease was strange, which added to the panic. There was no warning, it didn't matter if the person had been near or far from someone who dropped. There were only two outcomes. Either the person recovered within an hour, or they died. Like who got the disease, no rhyme or reason dictated the outcome. Strong men had died, frail old women had lived.

Frederick found a coat several sizes too big for him and wandered the city. The hunger raged in him, but he refused to allow even a tingle. After the battle with the aetheric and his close escape he had wandered the sewers. Then he'd left the stench and returned to the room he'd claimed as his own.

None of the clockwork he'd built on himself would come off. It had fused to him. He could repair or improve on it, but like the hunger in his soul, this would forever mark him apart from the rest of humanity.

The hunger lifted its head and growled as a woman carrying package crumpled to the street, her children cried over her, shaking their mother. Frederick saw her aether was all but gone. He walked close and concentrated on sending aether to her to no avail. Even when he crouched to put a palm on her forehead, he couldn't help. He barely had to struggle to restrain the hunger there was so little life left.

"I'm sorry," Frederick looked helplessly at the children. People moved away from them. A haze in the air caught his attention from the corner of his eye. He turned his head in time to see an old man in the middle of a crowd fall. Others collapsed, and the haze became more solid.

We hunt. The beast in him growled as Frederick threw out a net of threads. They passed through the haze sending barely a tingle. He needed another method. The haze fled down the street and Frederick followed. A woman at a water pump fell, Frederick didn't slow, but it gave him an idea. Instead of a net he formed a tube and sent it at the now reddish haze. It enclosed the thing and a sudden flow of aether made Frederick stagger and fall to his knees.

The woman behind him struggled to her feet and dragged her water bucket away empty. Frederick scanned the area but didn't see any of the haze.

He couldn't hunt something he couldn't see. From the stories he'd heard there must be dozens if not hundreds of them. Savagely he swatted at statue beside him, making it crumble. Running footsteps told him the crowd were fleeing the scene.

Frederick stomped back to his room and sulked. Something positive he could do with the hunger within him, and he had to rely on blind luck. To distract himself he worked on something he could use to defend himself against the swords the aetheric hunters carried.

They knew where he was and came directly at him, even when he was out of sight in the park. None of them had aether glass that he could see. How did they find him?

He made a shield made of steel blades. A heavy spring would force it into a disc, he tried to fit an easy way to return it to the shape of a single blade. Every attempt ended with him almost losing a finger to the shield's sudden deployment.

As he was ready to toss it aside as a failure, a hunch came to him. He made the turning cog thicker and added a ratchet lock. He could wind it shut then activate the shield with his thumb by moving the ratchet piece. It gave him a circular shield with a diameter of the length of his forearm. As he attached a holster for it to his waist, it felt right.

At least he could still build clockworks, though except for possible clients through Dan, there was little call for them. For amusement he built a little soldier which went through the first attack and defense. Making something with no sinister purpose was calming. He went through his stock of materials creating silly playthings.

Wouldn't hurt to check in with Dan. Frederick carefully wrapped his creations and headed toward the metal merchant's shop. The sun shone and warmed the cold metal on his body, even through the coat. There wouldn't be many more nice days before the rain and cold started. He didn't look forward to going through winter with brass, copper and steel fused to him. Frederick ran over possible solutions as he walked.

A disturbance behind him made Frederick spin and send out the aether tube before he thought about it. It caught a bit of haze which had been feeding on a child. His mother picked him up and hugged him. Enough aether remained for the boy to live.

He ruminated on the incident until he arrived at the metal shop.

"Hello, Dan?" Frederick called. No answer returned. Maybe he was in the back. Frederick put the bag of toys on the counter and walked through to the warehouse. He smelled Dan before he found him. A board beside him had writing Frederick couldn't read, probably Dan's own method for tracking his product.

The attack came without warning. It felt like something had taken a bite out of his heart. Frederick dropped beside Dan. The hunger in him whimpered, whatever hit him had hurt the beast as badly as

Frederick. He rolled to his back, but he already knew he'd face an immense red cloud. It lunged at him again and he put out his hand. The crystal pulled in enough aether for him to think clearly, but not enough to move.

The haze had no more intelligence than any wisp of smoke, but this cloud radiated malevolence, and worse, it showed the cunning of a hunting beast. It dispersed as Frederick watched, then lunged from his left, away from the crystal. The wires from the bracers gathered some aether, but not as much as the crystal had directly. He had to contain it, then drink it dry.

Frederick pulled in all his remaining aether. This would work, or he'd die.

Dying might be easier. The beast growled and snapped at him. *Live it is, then.* As the next lunge came Frederick formed a wall of red aether behind the cloud, he wrapped it around his back before the cloud could flee through the floor.

The cloud tore at him, shredding his soul, but each time it touched the wall of aether, strength flowed into Frederick. It wrapped tightly around him and tried to invade, but the touch of the crystals made it writhe in agony. Frederick thrust his right hand into the cloud, but even with the crystal in his palm and the wall, the cloud was stronger than him. Pieces of himself crumbled under the attack. His left hand brushed the holster holding the shield.

The shield sprung open with a clang, and Frederick put his right hand against it. Now instead of a thin thread pulled in by the crystal, the entire shield sucked in the cloud. The cloud screamed, wailed, even backed against the wall of aether behind it, but Frederick shrank the wall, forcing the cloud against the shield. The cloud fought to the last, but at last Frederick lay on the floor humming with the aether he'd taken from the thing.

"There's a void beast in the back. Feels like it just ate someone. Careful, this is a big one."

"Should we call for help?" The second voice sounded younger, nervous.

"Keep your shields up and you'll be fine."

"Yes, Castov."

Their footsteps echoed in the warehouse.

"Lord, this place stinks," Castov muttered. "The void beast must have caught a thief. Serves him right."

Frederick lay silent debating his options. They would be on top of him in seconds. Though he was fuzzy from the aether from soul stealer, it still wouldn't match the pair of trained aetherics. He rolled to his feet, as they came around the corner.

A red beam hit him, from the older one. The young one quavered for a second. Frederick still had the steel shield in hand he put it between him and the beam the loss of aether stopped before it began. He charged the pair. With the clockwork on his body neither of them had time to do more than reach for their swords. The shield connected with Castov's head making him reel back and fall unconscious. The beam snapped off along with a faint haze of red around the man.

So that's a barrier, easy enough. Frederick formed a shield just as a beam struck from the younger man. It splashed off the thin wall of aether between them.

"Look, you can fight me and die, or stop and we'll talk." Castov stirred behind Frederick, he pulled enough aether to make him lie still.

"You killed Castov." The young one drew his sword.

"He's alive, just look at him."

"What?" The aetheric stared at Frederick open mouthed.

"You can't see the aether in him?"

The young man shook his head and lifted the sword into attack position. "Never heard of such a thing."

"Now you have." Frederick leaned back against the shelves of metal. "How you track the void beasts if you can't see them."

"They disturb the aether."

"Interesting." Frederick rubbed his forehead. "Listen, just who are you people?"

"We're the Chosen." The young one straightened as he said it. "Only a few are born each year. We have the full ability to use aether. It is our duty to protect the aether blind."

"And keep it secret from everyone else." Frederick glared the young man. He had to be only a few years older than him.

"They would fear us, rebel."

"Like the builders a hundred years ago."

"They refused to aid the Chosen and were going to reveal our existence."

"Just how would builders aid these so called Chosen?"

"You stand there and ask that question?"

"You wanted the aether glass integrated into weapons."

"Aether glass?"

Frederick held out his right hand with the crystal on his palm.

"I've never seen something like that. What does it do?"

"Never mind." Frederick closed his fist. "Take a message to your commanders. I will hunt these void beasts. I propose a truce until they have been destroyed." He snarled at the young man, letting his hunger loose enough to make the aetheric pale and stumble back.

"You're the void beast who killed Antonov and Vassily." He raised his sword again and rushed to attack. Frederick pushed the sword aside with his shield, then put his hand on the young man's head and closed his fingers.

"I can also be the soul stealer who kills you, Castov, and every other aetheric I meet. Or we can have a truce, for now. Tell your commander." He pulled enough aether to drop the younger aetheric beside his companion.

Frederick looked around. There wasn't much metal in the warehouse. Most of the wooden shelves were dusty and empty. He tossed out a web of aether and created an army of golems from what metal remained. At the back of the shop, he found the drain to the sewer he expected.

Meet me here. Frederick gave them his order, *follow the flow to the exit into the river.* He wrenched the grate from the floor and made it a golem to follow the others. They walked into the hole, one by one. *Disturbed the aether?* Frederick bound a strip of cloth he took from the young one's jacket over his eyes, flipping the aether glass out of the way. He sat off to the side and tried to feel the aether.

I might as well try to feel the air. He stopped his hands from untying the cloth, instead of feeling the aether, he felt for changes, breezes which brushed across his face. The pair behind him were a gentle eddy. People walked by sending ripples behind them. The walls of the buildings and the cobbles of the street reflected them creating a web of information. There, something moved through the web, sending out its own ripples, but different than the ones passing on the street. This one absorbed as it moved.

Frederick took the cloth away from his face and blinked. Trying to fit the map of the aether with what he saw through the aether glass made him queasy for a moment, then it clicked into place. He headed out of the warehouse to hunt.

For the next week he hunted void beasts, or soul stealers as Katerin called them. The ones who survived to the end were huge, they hunted with great cunning and were as diligent in staying out of Frederick's way as he was determined to catch them.

The Chosen took out two, leaving the last cloud of evil alone. It fled from them and Frederick heading toward the one place none had been yet.

The Clockwork Circus.

***

Katerin sat in her room. If her friends had found her, they would have worried she was dead. She monitored the aether over the whole city. Anger made her push herself to dangerous extremes. Zirafia had run across the city, careless in spite of Katerin's warnings. She followed the path, not sure why, since she was too far to help if her cousin found trouble.

She heard Zirafia's cry, half vocal and half tear across the aether. Katerin's heart ached, and she had to hold herself in place with hands so tight that bones cracked.

Aetheric had found her, the worst of her fears.

Then it got worse. The soul stealer appeared. One aetheric was snuffed out, another wavered on the edge of death, but monster made so much noise she couldn't feel the already weakened aura of Zirafia.

There was something which may have been the gate opening, but how, if Zirafia was dead? Then the soul stealer vanished leaving no trace of her cousin. Other aetheric appeared. Katerin thought the weakened one died, but her concentration was broken by grief.

For the following days, she'd refused to leave her room ignoring all pleas or threats.

Lexburgh was overrun by soul stealers. She followed them by the felling of citizens until some grew large enough to stretch the web out of shape. They consumed each other as they attacked the city.

What she couldn't figure out was the soul stealer which waxed and waned in power, destroying soul stealers but leaving no other disturbance in its wake.

Then there were four, and after a battle which gave her a headache from its reverberations, there remained only one headed toward the circus, and the hunting one followed.

The augury slammed into Katerin like a club. She fought alone, surrounded by the corpses of her people.

Attacks came from all directions, and she weakened, falling to her knees, then the soul stealer showed up and she despaired.

Chapter 17 Breaking of the Gate

Katerin woke to stare at a cold white ceiling.

"You return to us." The headmistress leaned over her. "I was beginning to fear you wouldn't survive to take your punishment." She stood up straight. "Get strong, it begins soon. No more writing lines, my dear, that clearly has been ineffective. We will try something different."

Katerin tried to sit up, but leather straps held her to the bed, under the thin sheet she was naked.

Mischa came in after the headmistress had been gone for a full bell.

"I'm only allowed to stay for half a bell." Tears ran down her cheek. "When we heard you scream, we thought you had gone mad like Akilina. When the porters broke the door down, you were white as a ghost, they brought you here. Headmistress was furious. I've never seen her so angry."

"What happened to Akilina?" Katerin tried to sit up again, but Mischa pushed her down on the bed. "Relax, you aren't going anywhere." A cold gleam filled Mischa's eyes that Katerin had never seen. "Oh, yes, I could play the fool as well as any. There can only be two Chosen in a year. How curious that a girl came out of nowhere, so bright the people around were blinded by the light. You will tell us who, or perhaps, what, you are." Mischa put her hand on Katerin's head and cold weight pushed her down toward unconsciousness. "I will learn all your secrets, and how you are connected to that abomination LeSille."

Each time Mischa came, she asked questions Katerin couldn't answer. What was Frederick? Why was she involved with him? How did he become a void beast?" When Katerin couldn't answer, Mischa sent her back into unconsciousness.

***

Frederick stared at the wall of the circus. He couldn't detect anything on the other side. How could he have missed such a large gap in the web? But the aetheric hadn't realized either, not until now. They left one to watch, but otherwise life in Lexburgh went back to normal.

The citizens of Lexburgh flowed in and out of the gate like a river. He couldn't wait any longer. A day since the soul stealer had floated into the circus, who could say how much damage it could do?

But no one acted any different. The people in blue took coins, the circus goers eagerly entered, coming out hours later tired, but content.

Frederick chose a spot of the wall which separated him from a storage yard with canvas, posts and other things needed to build and repair the circus. He took a running jump to clear the wall, then bounced off a barrier which might as well have been brick.

He tried other places along the wall with the same result. Time to rethink his approach. Frederick went back to his room and the small army of golems which stood ready to obey his command, still stinking of the sewers.

Maybe that was the solution. The sewers ran under the circus as they did everywhere else. Frederick walked back to the hole in the building's floor he'd made to gain access to the sewers without going out on the street. He imagined the path of the sludge to the river and which direction the stuff from the circus would come from.

It took longer than he expected, but after wandering underground for the better part of a day, he heard the clatter of the circus above him. He climbed up and pushed a finger through the grate. There was a barrier, but not as strong as the one over the wall. Perhaps there to keep rats out. All the time he'd been there, he'd never seen one.

Back in his rooms he experimented with the golems until he could get a rudimentary feel for the web of aether through them. He didn't need all of them. Once the last soul stealer was gone, the aetheric would be coming after him. Frederick didn't intend to die by their hands even if they called themselves the chosen.

He counted forty-three of them, stationed about the city. Each had an individual flavour. On a whim he closed his eyes and felt for Katerin. She disguised herself very thoroughly as human, but he'd bet her aether would taste different.

She was safe at her school. Sleeping. *Sorry, but at least I saved your friend.*

He put her out of his mind and concentrated on his plans. A dozen of the golems he sent through the sewers to climb out of the grates and be his eyes within the circus wall. They would take most of the day to get into position and try to break in.

"The rest of you are out of luck." Frederick pulled the aether out of them. He wanted better protection than the few plates he wore. Steel flowed under his direction making armour which would allow him to move easily. Copper and brass became cogs and springs to work as extensions of his body. As much as the clockwork man-spider had upset him, he used it as a pattern. All of it hid under his coat, though it no longer fit loosely. Every bit of metal on him would feed aether to the crystal on his chest. He thought of that as where his hunger lived.

The first golems crawled through the grates as he adjusted his coat to fit better over his back. He sat and concentrated on them. The rubes followed the maze of streets to the big tent, then outward. They formed rough spirals with the hidden paths of the circus people between.

The golems stuck to the hidden paths, staying under the fabric of the tents, as they moved the flow of aether resolved itself. Bright lines leading to the show tent, then duller lines to the gate. A single strand of aether, the thickness of a tree trunk, led to a spot off to the side of the circus grounds. That thick strand glowed blood red.

Frederick sat stunned at the implication as one by one his golems vanished from his awareness.

The soul eater wouldn't have stood a chance. No wonder it was allowed in.

Now that he knew what the circus was, the question he had to answer was what to do about it. He'd been prepared to fight individual aetherics, but they paled compared to the trap of the clockwork circus.

Time to come up with a new plan.

Katerin's scream cut through his head and blinded him. He picked himself off the floor and reached out for her. All he found was pain. It came from where he'd saved that wonderful creature, midnight black and filled with the purest of light.

The aetheric wanted through the gate, and they were going to torture Katerin until she opened it. All the Chosen were gathered in the same spot, but there was twice the number. He hadn't thought about the girl's school.

The fabric of the web stretched, it would tear soon and the aetheric would flood into whatever lived on the other side of the gate.

At his command the clockwork golems went out on their last mission.

Frederick ran out to the street and jumped to the roof. He didn't have much aether, but he was headed to the biggest concentration of it outside the circus.

****

Katerin screamed as Mischa laid another reddish thread on her. It burned like fire even as it sapped her strength.

"Don't fight it." Mischa ran a hand across Katerin's forehead. "It is so much easier if you give in."

"H, how would y, you know." Katerin tried to snarl, but it came out a whimper.

"How do you think we learned?" Mischa turned to where the arch wavered and bent, one second showing the temple, the next inky blackness. "Almost time, and then your suffering will be done." She wove a net of blood-coloured threads and Katerin quailed at the thought of the pain.

"It won't take long, Akilina didn't last more than a few seconds, but then you're so much more powerful than her." Mischa licked her lips as the gate tore open. The aetheric men had their swords drawn, the women red glows in their hands. Katerin closed her eyes and waited for the pain.

The bonds holding her vanished as Mischa's dead weight fell over her. Katerin sat up, pushing Mischa off. A dart stuck out of the girl's neck with a thin wire running a few inches before it snapped off. Mischa had not the slightest spark of soul in her. Half of the aetheric had vanished through the gate. Some turned to face a new threat, while the rest dashed into the blackness.

The remaining aetheric had formed a wall facing outward. The soul stealer clung to a wall challenging them. A few bodies like Mischa's lay on the cobbles, but the rest either challenged the soul stealer, or ran amok in her home. Katerin picked up a sword from a young Chosen and ran through the gate.

Battle raged on the plains outside her home. The aetherics threw red soul stealer threads at her subjects. Her guards pushed them aside with balls made from their souls. Already some lay empty on the ground and the aetheric spread out and advanced, men and women paired. Even as she watched the aetheric grew stronger.

Life flowed into Katerin from her home, replacing what Mischa had stolen and more. She dropped her disguise and ran to attack the Chosen from the rear.

At first her charge shattered the careful order of the invaders, giving her guards time to fall back. But without the guards to fight, the Chosen turned on her. Katerin grinned at them, filling her sword with power.

They tried the same tactics on her that had worked well against the first line of the Phemeral defense.

Katerin was the queen of her people and she opened herself to the power of the Queen's stone, not the small fragment that Zirafia carried. She glowed like the sun in the Outer World blinding the Chosen, then she taught them that in the right hands, the soul force could burn.

They learned far too quickly, moving toward the city in a circle, the ones in the back taking the brunt of her attack, but bleeding the excess to the Chosen in the vanguard. Katerin cut off her attack and ran in a broad arc around the Chosen. She would stand with her people, and live or die as their Queen.

***

The Chosen were disciplined, Frederick had to give them that. Those who turned to block him, stood like stone. The darts were no longer effective; they needed surprise to work. Now they stood behind their barrier and fired bolts of red at him. Hooks meant to trap him and sap his strength.

He let them lodge in his shield, they focused, bore down on their attack. The Warden paced behind them calling advice and encouragement. If they kept it up, they would trap him and drain him dry.

The clockwork golems he'd sent out before he arrived crawled on the walls behind the Chosen. They jumped onto the Chosen, biting into arms, legs, whatever they could reach. Even as the aetheric swatted at them, the clockworks tripped and wires flew pulled by darts. These weren't aimed at the Chosen, so they ignored them as a failed attack. When the darts hit Frederick, they became a conduit for aether. Half of the ones the golems attacked died before they knew what was going on. The rest of the golems were crushed by the remaining Chosen.

The Warden shouted at the Chosen and they formed a tight clump. He put his hand on the back of the one closest to him and a brilliant bolt of aether leaped at Frederick. Most of it splashed off his shield but enough got through to lodge in him and draw his aether. The sudden loss made him dizzy, but the hungry beast in him took over and jumped at the group.

The extra limbs Frederick had added were meant for climbing and jumping, but from this distance they worked well as spears. He landed on the Chosen, impaling, stabbing, bearing them to the ground, and stealing their aether before they hit the cobbles.

The Warden stood between him and the gate, glaring at him with hate filled eyes.

"You won't get past me, and the rest will return from the underworld with more aether than you can imagine." He pulled his sword and stood ready to attack. "Try your tricks on me, builder."

Frederick stood and tossed away the shreds of his coat, then retracted the extra legs. They wouldn't do him much good in the tight space of the gate, where the Warden stood with a foot in either world. Aether flowed around and through him.

"Is this what you wanted?" Frederick waved at his body, more clockwork than flesh. "Combine clockwork and aether, make invincible warriors? Invade other cities to replace the population you've sucked dry over the years?"

"The Circus lied to us, said it would return for you when you'd graduated." Warden scowled at Frederick as if the Circus was his fault, maybe it was.

"My father was one of you, supposed to follow orders no matter what." Frederick took his shield out and activated it. "You helped him take the circus over, in exchange for me. What was I, an experiment to blend the abilities of aetheric and builder? Must have been disappointing to find out I couldn't use aether to save my life."

"Yet here you are." The Warden tensed.

"Indeed." Frederick walked forward casually, smiling at the Warden. "I must get my stubbornness from my father." He jumped forward and stabbed with a leg over his shoulder, but the Warden beat it aside, then attacked in turn. Frederick took the blow on his shield, pushing it away.

When the Warden lunged to stab at Frederick's heart he stepped into the blow and the sword screamed against the thick plate. The tip snapped off, but the Warden slashed the sword toward Frederick's neck. He blocked it with the shield reinforced with aether.

The next attack came against his armour, trying to twist it against him, but Frederick had sealed and shielded against that.

"You know that rule about not making golems too intelligent." Frederick smiled and stepped away from the next slash. "I'm guessing it has something to do with Katerin's people. Did they rebel against your ancestors? Like builders, were they too stubborn to bend?" He blocked two more cuts at his head. Without the assist from his clockwork armour, he'd have been dead twice over.

"They die like any other creature, and their children will be our slaves." The sword flew at Frederick, its speed boosted with aether. Frederick stumbled back, and the Warden brought the cut around so fast, Frederick couldn't see it. But he knew where it was aimed. It bit into his left leg with a clang and stuck. "That's been done." Frederick slashed with the shield cutting across the Warden's throat with the razor edge he extended for the purpose. His right hand landed on the Warden's heart and pulled the aether from him.

Frederick staggered from the inflow. He'd never held so much, and the beast howled for more. He ran through the gate into Katerin's world. The invading aetheric were far ahead engaged in a deadly battle with Katerin's people. He found her by her brilliance brighter than anything he'd imagined possible. The battle was turning against Katerin. The Phemeral couldn't or wouldn't use the soul stealing threads, so one by one they fell.

He hit the back of the aetheric wedge like a boulder, crushing the invaders before they knew he was there. The last few standing he snatched their lives, not needing the red aether anymore.

"Frederick?" Katerin ran to him, beautiful as obsidian and diamond. "How, why?" She looked around. "It doesn't matter, we've won."

"Not yet." Frederick sighed. "This was the easy part."

Chapter 18 The Clockwork Circus

The ground shook and Katerin went to her knees. Frederick stood staring back at the gate, tears running from his right eye. Impossibly he had a piece of the Queen's Stone, or something very much like it over his other eye. Another fragment glowed on his hand.

"Sorry Katerin." Frederick put up his right hand and began to draw strength from her people. They fell to the ground and lay still. She attacked him, but he froze her in mid-air then drew the power of the Queen's Stone through her. Throughout her land her people fell as the stone which sustained them suddenly became an enemy. She screamed and railed at him, cursed him, then begged him as her augury came to life around her.

A figure too small to make the earth shake strolled toward them. Baelophile, the Ringmaster. He shone so bright with bloody aether it made Katerin ill. When Frederick put her gently on the ground, she could only vomit into the dust.

"Well, son." Baelophile's words were painfully loud. She put her hands over her ears and wished for death. "It's about time we talked."

***

"Father." Frederick responded. He made the word a curse. This was the man who'd forced him to betray the only person who'd ever shown him kindness. "Still sending others to do your dirty work."

"Oh, this is me, just as Gears, Skattigrim, even cute little Lylphy with her crush on you are all me. I am the Clockwork Circus, but it is so much trouble to move, I sent a baby finger to deal with you."

"You may find I'm not that easy to handle."

Baelophile laughed, the sound flaying Frederick and vibrating his armour.

"I could have sent Lylphy, and you would still lose. I am the most powerful being in the world. I've been drinking souls for millennium, since before the Phemeral rebelled and made their escape with their precious stone. Most of it anyway. A few chips fell here or there. Useful things, bait to turn wayward sons into soul stealers."

"I guessed as much when I saw what you were."

"Your pathetic golems, like rats spying on me. Nothing happens in the Circus without me allowing it."

"You wanted me scared, ready to bow down and make a deal, anything to stay alive." Frederick walked forward to meet the Clockwork Man. "The Warden could have told you I have a problem with obedience."

"The Warden, he was enraged I returned before his plan could come to fruit. It wouldn't have mattered, but I grew bored wandering the wastes. Drinking life from peasants and farmers."

"I suspect when you left, he started working to become you. The aetheric were already a lie, why not make them soul stealers too?"

The laugh slashed at him again. And a flip of Baelophile's hand sent Frederick crashing into the rocks.

"He could have used the entire city and not touched me." Baelophile threw Frederick against another rock face.

"Full of yourself, aren't you?" Frederick coughed up blood, but forced himself to his feet.

"I can give you the circus, all those precious friends you made. Yours."

"I don't live off the life of my friends." Frederick shot the words like arrows at Baelophile.

"But here you've sucked an entire world dry," Baelophile smirked. "You don't have many friends do you? But you've done me a favour gathering all the aether here for me. With this I won't only own the city but the entire land, maybe the world."

"I won't give it to you." Frederick crossed his arms.

"Ever the stubborn boy." Baelophile stretched out his hand and pulled.

Frederick went to his knees and laughed, as the aether went out of him, he lost control of the clockwork he'd had a golem place very carefully.

The aetheric energy of Katerin's world blasted up from the sewer through the tent where Owner sat in darkness and drank the life of the world. It vapourized him before he could react. Baelophile staggered and put his hand to his head. He looked up with black rage in his eyes.

"I told you, I am the circus. You destroyed one piece, one cog, since you're a builder." Baelophile reached out again. "I am still going to suck you dry, then I will empty your city, destroy this world. With the stone the Phemeral have, I don't need you." He pulled Frederick into his hand.

"As you said, Circus, I'm a builder." Frederick gasped the words past Baelophile's grip. "A grain of sand in the wrong place can stop a clockwork dead." The bolt of energy curved down to slam into the huge mainspring of the great wheel. It exploded sending steel slicing through the circus into the big tent where Skattigrim was just introducing their newest act on the high-wire. The poles snapped and Lylphy screamed as she fell from the wire.

Baelophile went to his knees gasping, the massiveness which had surrounded him dissipated like mist. He dropped Frederick to the ground. With the last bit of life in him, Frederick slashed the shield towards Baelophile's neck. The Clockwork Man sent a thread to pull the last trace of aether from Katerin. Frederick caught it and stopped it short, but the thread sucked him dry. His mind went blank, and he toppled forward.

***

Katerin had never hated anyone the way she hated Frederick. Her people were dying around her, and he walked out to meet that monster. For all the destruction he'd caused, it wasn't doing him any good as Baelophile threw Frederick around like a rag doll. With all the power he'd stolen, he should have at least put up a fight.

She forced herself to her feet, and using the sword as a cane, hobbled painfully toward them. Each second she grew weaker, knowing more of her people died, but she would not leave them unavenged.

Then Baelophile swayed like he'd been dealt a heavy blow, though Frederick was on hands and knees on the ground. The invader pulled Frederick to him and held him ready to crush his throat. Katerin would have urged him on, only then he'd turn to her.

Another blow hit Baelophile knocking him to his knees. Frederick moved to attack, but a red thread flew at her. She couldn't dodge it or block it. She was dead.

It stopped short of her. Frederick held it in his hand until the life went out of him.

Baelophile pushed Frederick off him and lay on the ground laughing.

He stopped when she drove the sword through his heart.

Katerin fell to her knees, the last of her kind, but not for long. She lifted her head to bid farewell to her slaughtered people before she died.

A bolt of light blew through the gate and struck her. It carried her to the rock face where aetheric and Phemeral lay motionless. Pinned against the rock Katerin screamed until her voice gave out.

It felt like eternity before the aether dropped her to the ground.

Life flowed in her and she wailed at the irony of being too late.

"My Queen." A guard fell to his knees beside her. "The people are scared and confused. We need your guidance."

"You live?" Her voice was barely a rasp.

"We do, I know not how." The guard lifted her. "You must come to the Hall of the Chair and address your people."

Katerin stood on shaky legs.

"Help me over there." She pointed to where Frederick and Baelophile lay. The guard waved another over and they carried her to Frederick.

"I don't know if this will work, but you aren't escaping that easily." Katerin reached for the Queen's Stone. It still reverberated from the impact of returning life force. Then she put her finger on the stone in Frederick's hand and sent a bolt of aether into him. She thought of all the times Vassily had stopped his heart, and she had healed him, again and again.

"What would have happened if I'd let you die?"

***

Frederick opened his eyes to see Katerin's diamond eyes staring down at him with flashes of green in their depths.

"How many times have you saved me?" His voice was a whisper, then he coughed on blood and couldn't breathe. Katerin's hand lay cool on his forehead and the coughing eased.

"I'm not sure if it's one times too many, or not enough." She sat back on her knees.

"You're so beautiful, like your friend." Frederick whispered. "I made sure she made it home."

"Zirafia." Katerin's face brightened. "She lives?"

"My Queen, she came and warned us then took her people and left into the mists."

"It will be long before we meet." Katerin pushed herself to her feet. "Bring him along. Bury the other with the sword still in his heart."

They walked to the city of the World Beneath, not near as big or grand as that above, but Frederick turned his head to admire the people and their homes.

"What are you looking at?" Katerin asked finally. "I know there is no light for humans to see by here."

"But there is life." Tears glistened on Frederick's cheek. "I wasn't sure, but I hoped, your life would find you."

"You can see their souls?"

He put a hand to his left eye. "The aether glass lets me."

Weeping came from a home, then others.

Frederick's heart wrenched, and he would have fallen if the guards hadn't held him. Katerin's face was stone and her eyes glittered. But she greeted each who came to her with a touch on the heart.

They came to the heart of the city, more a more a mansion than a palace. Guards saluted her as she passed, but here their faces were solemn. Frederick's heart sank further. When they entered a large room in the center of the mansion, the people moved out of Katerin's path. Frederick saw a woman in the chair. She sat erect, proud, but no life flowed through her, something lay still on her lap.

"Mother," Katerin whispered and ran to the chair.

"Put me down here." He rasped to the guards. "I'm not going anywhere."

While Katerin grieved, Frederick took stock of the damage. More of the metal had fused with his body, what hadn't was a twisted mess, making movement all but impossible. If he'd had some aether, he might have been able to set some of it to rights.

He could see through the aether glass, but the stone in his palm was cracked and lifeless, as if the little aether Katerin sent through it had finished it.

The beast in his soul lay quiet, but he couldn't tell if it was dead or sleeping. For now, he was a prisoner in his own body.

Chapter 19 Joining the Circus

Katerin thought her heart would shatter from her grief. Of all the people to have died. She brushed her mother's hair away from her face.

"I'm sorry, Mother." Katerin whispered. The pain of speaking felt appropriate, as if she should pay for all her mistakes. "I still don't know if I did the right thing, I even brought him to back to life, again." She bowed her head and buried it in the robes on her mother's legs.

"Your mother was never anything less than proud of you." Her father put his hand on her shoulders.

"But she's dead because of me." Katerin raised her tear covered face to her father. "If I hadn't saved him..." She couldn't finish the words and began sobbing again.

"Your mother sent you to watch him." Her father knelt and put his arm around her. "She saw pain and grief if you did. She saw she wouldn't live to the turn of the year if you did. But she sent you anyway."

Katerin turned to him. "Why? Why would she do that?"

"If the one you watched died, or if his life was too easy, our world would have stayed safe here in the Beneath." Her father squeezed her shoulder as she tried to make sense of what he was saying.

"But she sent me knowing she'd die. That's why she made me Queen so suddenly." Katerin shook her head.

"If we'd stayed in the Beneath, the circus might have taken over Lexburgh. Thousands would have died, the rest would become slaves to feed the circus' appetite. Evil would have sat over us until one day it discovered the gate." He shook her gently. "We would have fallen immediately to that power, become its servants. In time we would be as evil as it was. Remember, we went into exile to remove ourselves from the temptation of ruling a weak and foolish world. In doing so, we defied our creators, and they cursed us to be always choosing between our life and the lives of those we would save."

"I don't recall it being taught quite that way." Katerin pushed herself to her feet. "But I understand, if we lived easy while others perished, we don't deserve our lives." The touch of the stone flowed across her, healing her body's wounds. Her heart ached, but as much with pride for her mother's courage as in grief.

"We will bury the Queen Past with all ceremony, Harmo will rest with her as he did in life." Katerin spoke to her people. "Then we will find a way to live with the Outer World. We will defy the Makers again, and become, not rulers, but healers."

Guards lifted her mother from the chair, wrapped her in her robes, then hoisted her to their shoulders to carry her from the room. Every Phemeral in the room knelt in homage. When they'd passed the door into the hallway. Katerin sat in the chair. Through the Queen Stone, she touched every Phemeral in her realm. She eased their hurts and shared their gift.

When she'd returned to herself. Katerin sat alone in the hall.

"You gave me the hard part, Mother, but I think I'll be all right now."

***

Frederick sat nervously as the Phemeral smiths cut away the layers of armour which trapped him. He kept expecting to feel pain when the saws started. But it was only dead metal. They took four days to get to where they couldn't take any more away. The plates and armbands were part of his body. He felt touch on them as if they were skin. Nothing else, no flow of life through him. Part of him missed the intoxication of the aether, another part dreaded its return. The aether glass had replaced his left eye, and it still let him see the web of souls around him.

Once he could move again, Frederick set to repairing the damage to his legs. All the gears and extra springs to let him move and jump with the aether had been removed, leaving him with bare bones of steel. The place on his left leg where the

Warden's sword had stuck looked weak. He cut it off and remade it with the help of the Phemerals.

In the frenzy of preparation for battle he hadn't hesitated to let go of his frail leg of flesh and bone, but now he missed it, another piece of his humanity gone.

From the conversations around him, the almost death of their entire people had been laid at the feet of the invaders. Their queen had saved them by putting a sword through the heart of evil. None of them were sure where Frederick fit in, but they treated him with respect and courtesy because the queen asked it.

He had no intentions of trying to explain. Some days he felt like the saviour of the Phemerals, others like their murderer.

When he had done enough work to allow him to walk again, Frederick had the Phemerals guide him through their home. They pointed to sights and talked about their long history. He quickly learned they lived much longer than the humans above. Katerin, he was told, had lived for centuries of his world's time. Frederick didn't know what to make of it. So he accepted it and moved on.

A couple of days after he'd started walking, the queen summoned him to the hall.

"Hi Katerin." Frederick waved, and the guards growled as they moved toward him. She waved, and they stepped back. "Right, you're the queen." He tried to kneel; but ended up falling over and the guards had to pick him up.

Katerin's mouth twitched. "You may leave us." She waved the guards out of the room. "I think I'm safe enough." Then her eyes caught his and held them. Frederick counted his breaths to keep from speaking and making a bigger fool of himself. "Bring a chair over and sit down." A smile crossed her face.

Frederick moved the chair without falling over, then sat in it and sighed.

"Walking is a lot harder when the metal is dead."

She tilted her head. "What do you mean?"

"The aether flowed through the metal, it moved like part of my body, only stronger, faster. That's the only reason I'm alive." His face burned. "One of the reasons. Why did you bring me back? I was quite content to be dead, as long as he died first."

"Sorry, but you left him for me to kill."

"So I heard, you're their hero queen. They'd do anything for you."

"Are you disappointed you aren't the hero of the story?"

"I don't think I am the hero. I did some horrible things that are going to trouble my sleep for the rest of my life. Your people aren't the only ones who suffered from my revenge on my father."

"I know, the city is in chaos because most of the ones who knew how to run it are dead. The remaining aetherics want to be in charge, but as you know, they aren't the brightest."

"Another crime the Chosen committed." Frederick growled. "They created the aetheric class, then hid amongst them. The entire academy was intended to teach the chosen for each year. None of the rest had a clue."

"Our healers think they tampered the with aetherics at birth, any who showed too much intelligence met with accidents or were driven mad." Katerin frowned. "There are a few Chosen left, the Lord Mayor, the very young and the very old. We're hoping with better education we might make the younger ones more human."

"Better you than me." Frederick put his hand out. "I've had more than enough of them."

"But that's not why I asked to speak to you."

"I was informed you commanded my presence."

Katerin laughed, and Frederick's heart eased a little.

"It's good to hear you laugh." He looked down. "After what I did, I can't imagine why you brought me back. You didn't answer me the first time I asked."

"It's simple, or extremely complicated." Katerin rubbed her forehead. "The simple answer is because I'm a healer, and I will always choose to give life over death, almost always." She stared at the ceiling and Frederick admired how she had changed to become more regal, but then again, she'd always had a bit of that quality to her. "The complicated reason," Katerin looked over at him, "requires an understanding of our history. We defied our makers—"

"I was right, you are the reason it's forbidden to make golems intelligent."

"We are not golems." Katerin frowned in distaste. "But you are right, it is all people remember of us. I doubt there is the knowledge or power to create beings like us again. I think that is no bad thing. When we rebelled, there was an argument among us whether we should withdraw: or stay and rule those who'd made us. They decided staying would make us as bad as the ones we'd fought. Thus we left and spent centuries in peace finding out who we were as people." She laughed at herself. "Listen to me. The truth is, we struggled and fought, some became soul stealers and others destroyed them. It was the Queen Stone which saved us. They had damaged it in the final battle with the makers, but we brought it here and what pieces we could find. Zirafia wears the largest such fragment on her hand. The more the Stone joined us, the more painful it was to fight each other. The soul stealers became legends, monsters to scare children in ghost tales. Some stayed in your world to become dark creatures in caves. I'm sure the circus began as one of my people."

"Then the queen, my mother had a vision that if a certain human was watched over, we might all die, and certainly many of us would. She sent me to watch you, knowing as a healer, I would protect you and keep you alive."

"Even though I was your sworn enemy?" Frederick leaned forward.

"You remember that?" Katerin looked down.

"I remembered it when I saw the green flashes in your eyes."

She sighed. "I saved you, but I didn't want you to know. I didn't want you to like me."

"Because I was your enemy."

"Because I was afraid to be your friend." Katerin put her hands to her face. "I saw every day how much pain you were in, but I could only do so much. If I was your friend, it wouldn't be enough."

"It was enough." Frederick pushed himself upright and clumped up the couple of steps to clank to his knees beside her. "It was more than enough. Even at my angriest, at my most hateful, I held back because of you. I knew you wouldn't like what I was doing. I didn't like it, but anger drove me, and the need to feel the aether flow through me." He dropped his head on the arm of her chair. "I don't deserve life."

She put her hand on his head, and it felt like it always had, gentle, caring, understanding. Frederick's heart broke and sobs wracked his body. He saw the faces of the dead, even those he'd hated, and regretted their deaths.

"They shaped you as much as you shaped yourself. In the end, you fought for life. The last thing you did before you died was save my life." Katerin brushed at his tears. "You are not a monster, just human."

"You said your mother knew I would cause all this, yet she sent you to protect me?"

"My father told me." Katerin brushed his hair with her fingers. "She could ignore your need and have peace now; but leave our descendants to face horrific evil. Or we could face the pain and evil now; and hope to leave our descendants a better world." She patted his shoulder. "My mother chose to suffer now, to save the future. Not just our future, yours too."

"The Clockwork Circus," Frederick lifted his head. "No one could have stopped it."

"Even the Clockwork Circus wasn't all evil. It fed off people, but it gave them something in return, a vision of a different world. Maybe if a different person ran it, but it chose people who were greedy and power-hungry." Katerin picked up something and played with it in her fingers. The flower he'd bought her that one wonderful day.

"What happened to the Circus?" Frederick closed his eyes. "The last thing I saw was Lylphy falling. She was the grain of sand to stop the works. When Skattigrim saw her fall, he stopped the show, the high-wire made the collection of aether possible, but without him, it stopped. She was innocent and friendly, though part of the circus. Another person I killed."

"The Circus is in confusion. All their clockworks stopped, Skattigrim won't leave Lylphy's side to run the show, and no one else can."

"She's alive?" The hope in Frederick's heart was more painful than the grief.

"I just got the message today. One of our healers is working on her, but they're afraid she'll never walk again."

"I must go see her. Maybe I can do something. Please, my queen." Frederick bowed his head.

"When did I become your queen?" Katerin voice sounded odd.

"I think you've always been my queen." Frederick put his hand on his heart. "You always will be."

"I was thinking you'd want to go." Katerin's voice was soft. "I will send you as my loyal subject."

"There's only one thing I need you to do." Frederick looked up at her. "I need help to get up."

***

Frederick knocked on the gate, and Gears opened it.

"Brass." He pulled Frederick in and shut the gate behind him. "Am I glad to see you. Nothing is working in this place. Baelophile is missing, there's a hole in the ground where Owner's tent was, the big wheel's mainspring destroyed everything in its path. And the roughnecks, it's like they've forgotten what they're supposed to be doing. The callers are almost as bad. None of the performers will move from Lylphy's side."

"Baelophile won't be coming back," Frederick said. "He got greedy and ran into trouble with the aetheric."

"He did like to throw his weight around. Always figured himself the next Owner."

"Who's running the place now?"

"No one." Gears threw his hand in the air. "I've been telling you that. It's all falling apart. It's been downhill since Owner banned you."

"Well, I'm back. Let me see Lylphy, then I'll help you with the clockworks."

"She'll be glad to see you. The girl's been moping, saying she fell on her first show."

"Anyone would fall if the whole thing collapsed under them."

Gears stopped and looked over at him. "How'd you know that?"

"Healer told me."

"You know him?" Gears raised his eyebrows. "Strangest looking person I've ever seen. Black as night and eyes like the stars."

"Gears, you're a poet." Frederick clapped the man on the back. "We have a mutual friend."

The other man shook his head; but headed off toward the wagon yard. He pointed to a brightly coloured wagon.

"She's in there. I can't hardly look at her. She used to follow me everywhere, like she did with you. Isn't a person in the circus who doesn't like Lylphy."

Gears turned and walked away, his eyes glistening.

Frederick sighed and stomped over to the wagon. He'd got walking down all right, but stairs were a challenge.

"What did you do to have Owner ban you?" Svad came around the corner and frowned at him.

"Owner was my father." Frederick leaned against the wagon. "He left me to rot when he joined you, then comes back and wants me to be 'Yes, sir, right away, sir.'" He clenched his fist, the bits of plate still attached squeaked. "Been meaning to oil that."

"Owner's son?" Svad stared at him. "We was here just more than twelve years back. He come on then." He shook his head. "What did he want that was so terrible?"

"Asked me to betray a friend." Frederick pushed himself away from the wagon and looked into the distance. "Looks strange without the wheel."

"Don't change the subject." Svad came over and smacked his leg. "Ow, I thought that was your real one."

"Don't have a real one now," Frederick kept looking away. "Did something stupid and lost the other one."

"Well then, how are you going to wrestle if you don't have either leg?"

"We'll figure something out, Svad."

"Your friend all right?"

"Is now."

"That wouldn't be the nice-looking girl you came with the first time you showed."

Frederick looked down at Svad. "How do you know that?"

"Owner had us watching for you. Didn't say you were his kid. Not even sure I know how we knew it was you. Kander slipped a message from Owner to you at the show. He was a slick one."

"Was?"

"The mainspring did a lot of damage, we were lucky it wasn't worse. When Lylphy fell, Kander ran out to catch her. Saved her right enough, but broke his neck doing it. Lylphy's blaming herself. So with that and not being able to walk..."

"I'll talk to her."

Svad peered up at him. "And what make you think you can say something the rest of us can't?"

"Because I know what it's like to die to save someone you love."

"That girl?"

"Something like that." Frederick shrugged. "Turns out she's a bit older than me. She's more like my sister now."

"Ouch." Svad stopped himself just before he slapped Frederick's leg again. "You said you died. But you're standing here, right as rain, mostly."

"I did die, because it would be a better world with her in it."

"Who brought you back then?"

"She did, she's a healer."

"You're even, then."

"No Svad, we aren't even, not even close. It's going to take the rest of my life to pay that debt."

"Ah."

Frederick listened to the circus. It was quiet without the noise of the clockworks and the shouts and bustle of the rubes.

"I think you should go have a chat with our Lylphy."

"Was planning to, but I have a problem with stairs."

"I can hoist you up if you don't mind."

"I'll never complain about help from a friend."

They walked over to the wagon, and Svad hoisted him up to the top step.

Frederick raised his hand to knock, then hesitated. Would she really want to see him? Maybe she'd look at him and know it was his fault, that everything was his fault.

The door opened and Skattigrim stared at him, his hair a tangle, and clothes wrinkled, then he stepped back. "It took you long enough."

"I had some things to work out."

"Don't we all. The world isn't the same place it was a week ago."

"I came to visit Lylphy." Frederick fumbled out the words.

"I didn't think you were here to see me. Lylphy's only been asking to see you a dozen times a day."

"Let's not keep her waiting."

Frederick followed Skattigrim into the wagon, then into a room at the end. The enormous bed almost swallowed Lylphy.

Skattigrim sat in a chair in the corner. "I'll rest here a while. Sekila is cooking for the roughnecks."

"Brass!" Lylphy sat bolt upright in bed. "You came. I knew you'd come." She pulled out Taffi. "She stopped working."

"Let me take a look at her." Frederick clumped over and sat in the chair beside the bed. He took the clockwork and peered in at her works. "Mainspring's shot. I don't have one with me, but I can get one and she'll be good as new."

"Good, at least *she'll* be all right." Lylphy arranged Taffi carefully beside her. "What happened to your other leg?"

"Did something stupid and lost it." Frederick slapped the metal. "Svad's mad because he thinks I can't wrestle with two fake legs."

"You could hardly wrestle with one good leg." Lylphy frowned at him. "What makes you think you can do better now?"

"There's only one way to find out."

"Svad's going to throw you all over the place."

"Probably."

"You'll hit your head again."

"Possibly."

Lylphy stared at him as her eyes filled with tears.

"I killed Kander, Brass."

"I heard it he ran out to save you."

"And now he's dead."

"He loved you." Frederick said. "He'd do anything to protect you. Even die if he had to."

"It's not fair." Lylphy wailed. "He shouldn't be dead."

"It isn't fair." Frederick looked down. "But I know how he felt. That if he didn't do everything he could, *everything,* then he couldn't live with himself."

"How do you know?" She dragged herself over to him, her legs a dead weight behind her. The aether flowed in them, but so much weaker than the rest of her body.

The sight of them stabbed like a knife in his heart. Tears squeezed out of his eyes.

"Brass?" Lylphy sounded uncertain. "Brass are you all right?" She wrapped her arms around him. Her sobs shook him, but he only put his hand on her head until she stopped. "Brass." She said into his chest. "Tell me how you know."

"There's a girl, Katerin. I never knew her well, but she was always kind to me, always." He sighed. "I wasn't always that nice back, but I was angry, confused."

"You didn't sound angry and confused when you were here." Lylphy tried to sit up, and Frederick helped, making sure she was secure and comfortable.

"Being here with the circus, that was the best time of my life." Frederick picked up Taffi and turned her around in his hands, then put her down. "I had friends, I fixed things, the world made sense."

"But Owner banned you. I wanted to go and talk to him, but father wouldn't let me."

"Owner wasn't a nice person. He wanted me to hurt people, and I did, I hurt a lot of people." Frederick took a shaky breath. "I hurt you. But I refused to hurt her. I couldn't, so I fought until I couldn't fight anymore. Then when he was going to hurt her, I stopped him. I knew I would die. I was fine with that. The world wouldn't miss me the same way it would miss her."

"You died?" Lylphy's voice squeaked.

"I did."

"But you're here now." She slapped his leg. "Ow. You aren't a ghost."

"She brought me back." Frederick put his hand on Lylphy's "She told me I needed to live to make up for all the things I did. I need to live a long time to do that."

"If you were dead, how did she bring you back?"

"She's a queen, Lylphy."

"Like in a fairy tale?"

"Just like a fairy tale."

"Why didn't she marry you, was it because..."

"It isn't that kind of fairy tale, Lylphy. This one's just beginning."

"Could she use her magic to fix me?" The hope in her voice hurt.

"If she could, she would. Believe me." Frederick closed his eyes and saw Katerin playing with the flower, watching it open and close. *You can do what I can't.* He hadn't believed her then. Now he wasn't sure. "She sent me."

"You can make my legs work again?"

Frederick shook his head and thumped his leg. "Ow." Lylphy laughed at him.

"Brass," her eyes opened wide. "Could you make me legs like yours?"

"Nope," Frederick grinned. "I'm going to make yours better."

***

"Full crowd tonight." Skattigrim peered out through the curtains. "Are you ready for this?"

"We've been working on it for months. She's ready." Frederick sighed and shook himself.

"I know she's ready, I asked if you were."

"Honestly, I'm terrified, but she will stun them."

"Right, let's get started."

Sekila checked Skattigrim's red jacket one last time, then planted a kiss on his cheek.

Skattigrim ran out into the circle, then tumbled and jumped, flying high to twist and flip, landing on a ball, solid as if it was the ground. Then to show it was real, he walked it around the ring.

"Ladies and Gentlemen, we come to you from far lands. Places where the Beneath touches our world and a little magic leaks out to lighten our lives."

The faces of the crowd stared at him entranced by his story.

"A clockmaker lived in that town. He was poor, his clocks made of wood and brass, but he'd seen the Queen one day, and she'd smiled at him. He fell in love, but knew it was foolish. She'd never love him back. Then one day he was out for a walk, and thieves jumped him."

Frederick walked out in bright pants and jacket, jaunty, but not rich. Thieves in dark clothing ran out and surrounded him. The men winked at Frederick as they took the tearaway leg of his pants away. He wore black beneath and hopped after them waving his arms. The crowd gasped and laughed until he went into a small tent.

"But being a clockmaker, he made himself a clockwork leg." Frederick walked out. He'd added gears and levers to his leg for the show. The story continued as he lost the other leg, then set out to get revenge on the thieves, but everything he tried went wrong.

"Then one day, the clockmaker walked about the town. The people hid when he passed because he looked hard and cruel." Frederick marched out into the ring and performers fled in all directions. The crowd booed, and yelled, as the story made the clockmaker more and more a villain.

"As he walked, thinking angry thoughts." The light shining on Frederick turned red. "He heard a cry. And far above him, the thieves had cornered the queen and were coming closer to rob her. She cried for mercy." Lylphy's voice rang through the tent. "But they wouldn't listen. She stepped back and lost her balance." The flood light showed Lylphy in a queenly dress teetering on the edge, then she fell. The audience screamed as Frederick ran forward arms outstretched to catch her. The lights went out. Lylphy landed safely on the bag and rolled off giggling softly. Then she arranged herself on Frederick's back before the lights came up.

"The clockmaker caught the queen as she fell, but the fall killed him." The crowd went silent, not sure what to make of this turn in the story.

"I'll not let you die, clockmaker." Again, Lylphy's voice rang through the tent. "You must do as much good as you have harm." She lifted Frederick up and pointed imperiously away. He knelt as she stepped back and out of the light.

"So the clockmaker took all his tools and set out into the world. Until he met a girl in a bed. Her legs wouldn't work, but the clockmaker set to work." Frederick tossed gears and springs in all directions, then a bucket of silver ribbons which covered Lylphy in the bed. When they landed the bed was empty.

"And now that you know the story, ladies and gentlemen, I present to you, for the first time in all the world, the Clockwork Princess." Skattigrim pointed up, and the lights jumped to show Lylphy high on the wire. A cage of silver and gold encased her body from the waist down. Her costume was silver and gold sequins to glint in the light. Frederick had used thin wires to move the aether from her body to her legs, the clockwork gave them support and strength. She couldn't move her legs much, even with the wires, but with the clockwork legs, she could dance.

Lylphy twirled and flipped, did cartwheels along the wire until the entire audience was on their feet.

***

"I have to admit, you did good." Svad stood beside Frederick watching with the rest of the circus people, Lylphy's magic high above. "But when are you going to learn to wrestle?"

"I'm working on it, Svad. One bit of magic at a time."

Lylphy finished as her father had by falling backward off the wire. Where his clockwork suit lowered him. She floated down on a thin wire, landing to thunderous applause. She bowed and waved before running into the wings. Gears had the clockwork animals in motion as Skattigrim introduced the next act.

Lylphy hugged Frederick tightly, then Svad for good measure, then Frederick again.

"Thank you, Brass." She leaned her head against him. "I never thought I'd perform again and here I am."

"It's just the beginning," Frederick said. "The whole world is waiting."

Alex McGilvery

Other books by Alex

Series:

Calliope Books
Calliope and the Sea Serpent
Calliope and the Royal Engineers
The Third Prince and the Enemy's Daughter
Calliope and the Kershan Empire

Spruce Bay Books
Wendigo Whispers
Cry of the White Moose
Disputed Rock

The Belandria Tarot
The Devil Reversed
The Regent's Reign
The Empire Unbalanced
The World Widens
The Fury Unleashed

Blue in Kamloops
Tranquille Dark
Columbia Smoke
Victoria Run

The Fae
Call of a Hero
Shieldmaiden's Quest

Stand-alone books:

The Clockwork Circus
Leedles and the Golden Tree
Generation Gap
The Gods Above
Tales of Light and Dark
Like Mushrooms (poetry and photography)
The Heronmaster
Blood and Sparkles, and other stories
Princess of Boring
By the Book
Sarcasm is My Superpower
Playing on Yggdrasil
The Unenchanted Princess

Read short stories and excerpts from his novels at alexmcgilvery.com